For Carolyn who has always s̲u̲p̲p̲o̲r̲t̲e̲d̲ ̲m̲e̲ ̲i̲n̲ ̲a̲l̲l̲ ̲I̲ ̲h̲a̲v̲e̲ wanted to do. Except perhaps canoeing.

Special thanks to Gillian and Ashley who have read, and re-read this novel almost as many times as I have.
Thank you both for your support and input.
Also, and especially to Suzanne who has pretty much edited this novel for me, without her input I would never have had the courage to publish.

About the author

Phil Watson left school aged 15 with no qualifications. His lack of academic achievement is adequately demonstrated throughout this novel.

This novel is entirely a work of fiction. The names characters and incidents are entirely the work of the authors imagination. All rights to this book are reserved

Tommy the Thinker

1

Tommy Flounders was lying in the dirt, under a run of rhododendron bushes. He was cold, wet and his bones ached like he had lived every one of his 71 years hard. Which for the most part he had.
He is, for a man of his age, in remarkable condition. Weighing a little over 15 stones (unless it was drugs Tommy did not do metric), 6' 1" tall, he carried very little fat.
True, his muscle had perished over the last 10 years or so, but he still attended the gym 3 times a week. He would happily fight men half his age. He could still run 5 miles and was physically active.
Dressed in thermal camouflage trousers, t-shirt, a Merino wool jumper and a camouflaged jacket. He had a tight fitting green woollen beanie (or dut as he had always called them) over his short-cropped salt and pepper hair. His face was streaked with camo paint. His boots worn and mud caked. Unless someone was looking for him, he would not be seen.
Born in 1950 Tommy was a man of his time, raised hard, in hard times. He understood from a young age that you 'never got owt for nowt' and for a family to survive, everyone had to contribute when they could. Whether this was putting money on the table for the family to live on, or bringing in food or goods from the back of a lorry, every bit helped. If you didn't work harder than you played, then times would always be tough.
His father, a shipbuilder turned steelworker, was also called Tommy. As men of his generation went, he was

considered a fair man. Rarely raising his hand to his wife Nancy and he never hit Tommy harder than he should have. He had spent 3 years fighting in the second world war, returning to a victorious country that was still no better off than it had been before the war.

If the family had to survive on ration books, then they would all be underweight. Tommy senior poached the Wynyard Estate just outside of the town. Mainly rabbits but on occasion trout and pheasant. He was also friendly with enough local sea fishermen to make sure the family ate cod at least once a week.

He had enrolled young Tommy into the local boxing club as soon as he was allowed. A man of few words, he had gripped his son by both arms, kneeling to look him in the eyes as he told him "A man has to fight for everything Tommy. If you are weak, you won't survive. You have to be able to use your brain and your fists, both are weapons. So, stick in at school and learn to fight. No bullying, mind you, but take no shit son."

'Take no shit son,' the words echoed in Tommy's head, as he reminisced.

Right now, lying in the cold, there is no doubt he would be more comfortable tucked up in bed but he was never more alive than at times like this. Even at 71, he relished putting everything on the line. Plotting, and executing a plan, he never felt more alive even in the winter of his life. He had fought for everything, and pretty much won every fight. More often, he had used his head rather than his fists, but he had accomplished much with both.

That said, this was his last time, no more after this. The ache in his bones he would feel in the days to follow, would remind him of his mortality and that there were others he knew, better suited to this kind of drama, and that would act on Tommy's behalf any time he asked.

He had promised himself on his 60th birthday that there would be no more hits and here he was, more than a decade later, a knife in his left hand pocket and a pistol in his right hand.

Tommy's pistol of choice is a No 1 Glock 17. Widely regarded as one of the best pistols in the world, the double stacked magazine holds 17 rounds. The gun barrel is good for 360,000 shots and the 33 parts that fit together to make the pistol, never fail, if it is well maintained.

Tommy had chosen hollow soft point bullets although, from the distance he would be shooting, any bullet would likely put a fist sized hole in its target.

A Glock was not easy to come by on the British mainland, but not impossible, if you knew the right people. Tommy had a book full of 'the right people.' He knew he would need 2 of the 9mm rounds that the pistol currently held.

It should be a simple enough task to carry out. When 'Big John Jameson' walked down between the side of the house and the bushes, to open the garage onto his Aston Martin DBX, Tommy would put one round in his back, stand, then put another in the back of his head. A classic hit.

It would then be a 5 minute walk, over the grassed garden and through a copse, to his car and a 50 minute drive back to Scarborough.

He was hoping there might just be enough of dawn to allow him to jog and shave a minute or so off his walking time back to the car. But better to be slow and sure, than to twist an ankle or knee hurrying.

There is no doubt that John Jameson deserved to die. Tommy had become aware of him through his IT team. A respectable business man to nearly everyone that knew him. John Jameson had a sadistic, evil side.

"He casts a shadow darker than Satan himself" Tommy had remarked, when he read the file that Terry Begley had presented him 12 weeks ago. Along with running a successful group of companies, John Jameson was a people and drug smuggler.

This was no big deal in Tommy's mind but what bothered him, what had made him decide to act, was that a lot of the people John Jameson smuggled went directly into the sex trade. Forced to work as prostitutes to pay off a debt that would never actually be paid. Some of these were children as young as 3 years old. That had signed John Jameson's fate.

2

The devil, thought Tommy to himself, is in the detail. He had always planned his illegal activity meticulously. Rough planning, carrying out weeks of surveillance, whenever he felt it was necessary. More recently, noting CCTV and ANPR positions and now, even these confounded doorbell cams that everyone seemed to think they needed.

Once he was happy with his plan, he walked it through a couple of times. Picked the date based on, in this case, the weather forecasts and the moon cycle. Now here he is, alert and feeling much younger than his age.

Tommy anticipated it would take the emergency services around 20 to 25 minutes to arrive at the property after the alarm was raised which, he thought would take at least 2 or 3 minutes from the first shot. After all, it takes a special kind of person to run recklessly towards gunfire, to investigate what was happening.

The only person here, other than big John, is his latest squeeze Tanya. If rumour is anything to go by, she will still be out of her head on smack for another 2 or 3 hours. Her phone activity, which had been hacked, rarely showed anything before 10am. So, it is unlikely she will raise the alarm. The nearest house is around half a mile as the crow flies, but people in the country are rarely concerned by gunshots. The chances are it will be a couple of hours, not minutes, before the alarm is raised and by then Tommy should be well on the way back to Hartlepool.

But if everything does turn to shit, he will have a minimum of twenty minutes before the filth arrive. By which time, he should have pulled away from his parking spot on a narrow lane, just off a road that runs across the back of the country estate and manor house that was John Jamesons current address.

Tommy knew that there were no CCTV or ANPR cameras between his parking place and the A64, which is the road he would use to take him back to Scarborough. In fact, he would drive past only 5 properties, and they were so far back, even CCTV would struggle to pick up his car, let alone the registration. Once on the A64 he should blend in with the daily commute, on a road that was always busy but, particularly so during the morning commute.

His car was a nondescript Ford Focus. The number plates were ringed with a car that sat in a long term storage garage at Heathrow. The legitimate car was insured and had an MOT so there was little, if no, chance of being stopped by plod.

If he was involved in an accident, he had a copy of the car owners' licence with Tommy's picture on it. In truth it was not a great copy but most people saw what they expected to see.

Tommy had embraced new technology, as it had come out, during the preceding years. Being one of the first to recognise the potential to make significant gains through legal, and not so legal, methods. Printing counterfeit driving licences was just one little perk.

Once back in Scarborough, Tommy would drive to 'Bernie the breakers' wreckers yard, on the outskirts of the town. Bernie was aware Tommy was coming and, when the £5K changed hands, the car would be compacted and stacked with the others in the yard, awaiting collection for the smelting plant. Tommy had known Bernie for a long time, and they were birds of the same feather. Bernie was as solid as a man could wish for, and would never mention what had transpired to Tommy or anyone else.

The Glock, the beautiful piece of engineering that it is, would be compacted with the car. The clothes Tommy was wearing for the hit and the blankets he was currently laying on, would be incinerated in front of Tommy's eyes. Fresh clothes were already at Bernie's as was, Tommy's current motor, a Bentley Continental.

Once he was satisfied with everything at Bernie's, he would jump into his Bentley and follow the coast road up to Whitby, before cutting over the Cleveland hills and back to Hartlepool. Born and raised in Hartlepool, he did not like being far away from the sea.

Tommy glanced at his Rolex Daytona, '£60k's worth of watch' he thought to himself, 'beats the Timex I got for my first watch.'

It was 03:12. In around 4 hours' time the deed would be done and for the last time, Tommy would make his well-planned escape. If, of course, there was no interference.

There was also a second operation going on that morning. It was being carried out by people that Tommy would trust his life with, which was just as well, as he was!

He thought back to how this life had begun.

3

At 14 he was running errands for Billy the Scouse who ran Hartlepool, Billingham and Blackhall. Billy was a class A bastard, a psychopath that really enjoyed hurting people. They had first met when Billy had sponsored a boxing night down at the town hall on the Headland. Tommy fought that night and was voted best boxer. At 14 yrs. old, he was 5' 11" tall and weighed just less than 15 stone, a freak of nature. He had a punch that would put any man to sleep.

There was a strong amateur boxing history in Hartlepool with boxers getting categorised by age and weight. That night, Tommy had been fighting a catch weight, luck of the draw tournament and ended up fighting a man 6 years older than himself, and 20lbs heavier, for a £5 winner take all purse.

Tommy was handsome lad with raven black hair, startling emerald eyes, that were surrounded by long almost feminine eye lashes. He could already grow a healthy stubble and his skin didn't carry the blemishes and spots that most fourteen year olds spent hours in front of a mirror worrying about. His body was gym hardened, his arms and shoulders way bigger than you would expect to find on a schoolboy, his belly flat and his legs stocky. He had a sharp wit and was softly spoken. Women and men gravitated to him socially and, for the girls, physically too. His mum always told him that her side of the family gave him his looks and his brains, whilst his father's side handed down his fists and his stubbornness.

After the boxing had finished that night, Billy invited Tommy to join him and his cronies for a drink in the Rising Sun, and they just seemed to hit it off talking boxing and football. That was also when Tommy first saw Billy for the man he was.

A couple of sailors had come into the Sun from one of the cargo boats that was in dock. They were loud and had had a bit too much to drink. One of them accidently spilled a little beer on Billy's brother Pete's shoes. Pete thought nothing of it, and the sailor had apologised, but Billy was having none of it.

Tommy could sense the change in Billy, his whole body seemed to stiffen and he tilted his head forwards looking up to look straight. His normal scouse whine became hushed and he picked his words carefully and precisely. Billy stood at just 6 foot tall, he was not a bulky man, he did not carry an ounce of fat but he oozed menace.

He walked over to the two sailors.

"Which one of you fuckers just ruined my brothers' shoes" he asked. Although not loud, his voice carried such menace that he got the attention of both sailors. and a number of regulars, who recognising Billy for who he was and what he was capable of, left the bar for the lounge.

One of the sailors put a hand on Billy's shoulder
"Sorry buddy, we meant no harm. Here, let me buy him a pint and you as well, for the bother"
"Those fucking shoes cost £10 and you want to buy us a fucking pint. You cunt!"
"Whoa hang on" the other sailor chipped in. He could sense the menace that Billy carried but was not afraid. "Calm down pal, this doesn't need to get nasty."
"The fuck it doesn't" Billy replied and with one swift move, he picked up an empty pint glass from the bar breaking it on the first sailors head before jamming the ragged sharp edges into the second sailor's right cheek, ripping it to shreds, but fortunately for the sailor missing his eye. The sailor screamed and bent away from Billy

trying to save himself from more damage. Billy dropped the glass and had landed 3 sickening blows to the first sailor's face before he had even thought to move, Billy always wore heavy gold sovereign rings. He liked to look flash but, also when using his fists, the rings protected his knuckles and served to tear the flesh of whoever Billy hit.
The sailor dropped from where he stood, unconscious before he hit the floor. Billy then began to kick him, aiming for his head. He just kept on kicking away, only stopping when the glassed sailor staggered to his feet with one hand holding his shredded cheek and the other resting on a table. Billy launched at him knocking him to the floor, sitting astride him and battering his head with both fists.
Tommy was gobsmacked and appalled. Tommy fought to win, and once he had won, he stopped. Billy fought to kill by the looks of things.
"Shouldn't we stop him?" he said to Pete.
"We can't," came the reply "he's uncontrollable when he is like this," fortunately the landlord of the Sun, Andy Goodman, was screaming at Billy loud enough to get his attention.
"Billy stop it, you're fucking killing him."
Something got through to Billy and he slowed his blows, slow enough for Pete to scuttle round and catch Billy's eye.
"Billy, we got to go before the fuzz get here. You've hammered these two."
The thought of explaining what had happened to the two sailors to the Police seemed to galvanise Billy.
"Right, you lot, fuck off for the night." He turned to the bar, looking at the few remaining customers. "You finger me and I will give you twice what these fuckers got." He

delivered the same message to the lounge, before running out, jumping into his car and disappearing.
The following night the Hartlepool Mail covered the incident on one of the inside pages. It said little other than 2 sailors had been involved in a fight in a local pub and that police were looking for witnesses. Most people in Hartlepool considered any sort of violence, that involved people from outside of the town, as their own fault and had little sympathy for them. Like most working class communities, they had a deep mistrust of the Police and would never help them. The truth of the matter was, by the time the papers hit the shops, the Police would have unofficially closed the case.
Tommy was unsure if he should see Billy and his gang again. He had no problem's having a ruck and even if it ever happened, taking a beating, but what had happened the previous night was sickening and uncalled for. Despite his misgivings, he decided to go out at the weekend and see how it went.
They met again the following Friday for a few beers and Billy was relaxed, even jovial. He only mentioned the 2 sailors once to say that one of the coppers, he had on the payroll, had told him both sailors were out of hospital and that their ship was due to sail the following morning, which would lead to the case being closed shortly afterwards.
Again, Billy and Tommy seemed to hit it off. When the fancy took him, Billy was a good listener and could even be charming. He asked Tommy about his family, what he wanted to do when he left school, his boxing and what else he did in his spare time. They moved on to the Gemini night club, where Billy was more than impressed when Tommy pulled a woman nearly twice his age. Just before Tommy left with the woman, Billy pulled him to one side. "Pop down the yard tomorrow Tommy, any

time between 10 and 12. I will be in the office. I want to talk to you about something."

4

The following day at 10 sharp, Billy arrived at Tommy's scrap yard, which was just off the main street in Graythorpe. He knocked on the door to the office. Billy stuck his head out and told Tommy to go wait in the workshop, as he had a bit of business to attend to. Tommy wandered over to the workshop where he stood and waited, looking at 2 half stripped cars, parts labelled and ready to be sold. Five minutes later, a hard faced looking woman left the office with Billy and they walked to where Tommy was waiting.
"Tommy, do you want a blow job before I send Cheryl on her way" he asked.
"Nah thanks" Tommy was quick to reply. Not wanting his cock anywhere near this woman not even just in her mouth.
 "OK then luv, on your way" said Billy smacking her arse, before he and Tommy went back to the office.
"Right to business" said Billy "you're a good lad and handy with your fists too. I like you son and that's more than I can say for most of the cunts I have on the payroll. I have work for you if you want it. It's not a regular job. Most of the time it's hanging around and going on the piss. When work comes along it's going to be giving some twat a slapping or collecting a debt. Are you interested?"
"Yeah Billy. Thank you."
The thought of putting money on the family table every week really appealed to Tommy. They ate ok but times were hard. A few extra quid a week would make all the difference at home.
Tommy was put on the payroll at £25 a week. £6 a week more than his dad earned for doing nights at the steel

works. Tommy explained to his mum and dad what he had been offered. His mum was firmly against it.

"The last time I spoke to one of your teachers Tommy, she said you were clever enough to go to university."
"University" his father responded his voice full of scorn. "How the hell is a working class lad from Hartlepool going to go to university woman. You're talking nonsense."
He turned to look at Tommy. "I know this guy Tommy, I know he is a villain, a wrong un. Are you sure about this son?"
"I know what he's like dad and I will be careful but think how much better it will be if I am putting £10 a week on the table".
His father stared hard at him. "OK son but be sure to be careful, jail time is hard time and you will be marked for life if you go down. No decent employer will touch you."
"No sweat dad, I will be careful. I promise."
So, it was settled. The 3 members of the Flounders family knew that Tommy was working for a gang leader, but cash was king in these hard times and boys had to grow up to be men way before they should.
Tommy had 6 weeks left before he could officially finish school but it was quite commonplace for young men to go missing during their last year, so he left and never looked back.
To earn his money, Tommy had to continue to train as a boxer and do anything else he was told. This mainly involved slapping the odd punter that got too far into debt in one of Billy's bookmakers or running parcels to the Turks over the other side of the river Tees with one of Billy's trusted men.
He enjoyed the trips to Middlesbrough. He felt trusted and useful. He knew if the Turks took issue with them, it would be no contest as they outnumbered, and no doubt

out gunned them, but it was still a rush for Tommy to be meeting real top level gangsters.

He also got to meet their leader, a guy called Omar. He seemed so sophisticated to Tommy. He had a big office at the back of a nightclub. He dressed fashionably in designer clothes and he was always clean shaven, smelling of exotic after shave, not Hi Karate that seemed to be the fragrance of choice in Hartlepool. When he spoke, everyone listened and despite Tommy only being 14, Omar treated him like an adult.

The first time Tommy met Omar, the Turk asked him a number of questions about his family and himself. How old he was; what he did for leisure; what he wanted out of life; how he had met Billy; did he enjoy doing what he did for a living? Not every question was easy for Tommy to answer. The fact that Omar had actually made him think, question himself, impressed Tommy no end. Every meeting since, however fleeting, he would always ask after the health of his mum and dad.

Omar made sure that Tommy was looked after, if the meeting was anything other than a handover of cash for goods. He made Tommy feel valued and important.

5

Along with being good with his fists, Tommy was also exceptionally clever and it was this that helped him quickly climb the ranks in Billy's organization. Tommy realised that there was only Billy that had any brains. The rest of the gang were just muscle, with no business or common sense whatsoever. Billy ran his mob ruthlessly. If he decided you were untrustworthy, the North Sea was a big resting ground and because of that, nobody would question his decisions, nobody but Tommy.

In 1966, when Tommy was closing in on 16, Billy decided to hit the Turks in their stronghold at the Middleborough nightclub that Tommy now visited every week. Animosity between Billy and the Turks had been growing over the past few months. The Turks were Billy's main suppliers of Marijuana, Opium and Acid, which were the drugs of choice back in the day and Billy's main source of income. Recently, the supply had begun to dry up. At the same time, a number of Turkish barbers had opened in Hartlepool and the paying public seemed to have no issues buying their drugs through these barbers. It was clear the Turks were testing Billy, moving in on his turf to see what his response would be. Billy had called his top boys together to discuss how to act. For Billy, it was all or nothing. There was no half way point, no compromise. He had already made his mind up on the plan. He would hit the Turks in Zanzibar's Night Club in Middleborough, which was their stronghold and the centre of their money laundering operation.

Billy, Sidney one toe (nicknamed because of the webbing between his toes), Irish Alf, Bobby Campbell, Smooth Simon (the ladies' man) and Billy's brother Pete were sat around a table at the Station Hotel. The pub was closed with curtains drawn. The room heavy with tobacco smoke and the smell of stale booze. Tommy was also there, his job was to make sure the lads' glasses were never empty, and to do anything else he was told. Despite being recognised as a member of the gang, there was still a pecking order and because of his age, Tommy was bottom of it.

Billy outlined his plan, which was as simple as hitting the club hard around 1 am on Saturday morning. The 6 of them, plus another 20 or so casual gang members that could be called on for a tear up, as and when necessary. Billy said that they would arm themselves with baseball bats, razors, knuckledusters and knives. In quickly and hard, seeking out the Turk mob and giving them the pasting of their lives. Causing as much damage as possible to the club before returning to Hartlepool. Everyone agreed it was a great plan.

Tommy, who had been listening, thought that not everyone might really agree but nevertheless, there was not one single voice of dissent.

"We will wear balaclavas" said Billy, "no one will know it was us. We will be home in bed, banging the missus, before they even wonder what hit them" he said, downing his 5th pint of the day.

Tommy thought hard. He loved working for Billy. The money was more than useful at home and a recent pay rise had meant he was earning more than double of anyone in his family. Putting money on the table, contributing to the family, meant a lot to him.

He knew if he said something to Billy that was not taken well he would, at best, be out of favour. With a beating and no job. At worst, taking a fishing trip, as Billy called the fate that befell the people that most pissed him off. However, he could not restrain himself.

"Billy," Tommy asked, "what about the cash?"

Billy sighed. "Fuck sake Tommy! Do I need to spell everything out? Of course, we will empty the tills. Every fucker knows that!" The table mumbled their agreement. Some grinning at the boy's foolishness.

"Yeah, I know" said Tommy "but I meant the drugs cash. If you take that, and you give anyone there a smacking, you also get compensated for the lost sales."

"What the fuck are you on about?" was the terse reply. The menace in the voice was clear. The table was quiet. No eyes on Billy, all on Tommy

'Shit or bust,' he thought, before saying,

"Well, if you went in at 3 am, the club would be empty of punters. Only maybe ten Turks left. You could hit them hard, take the night's takings and, if you get into Omar's office, any drugs money too. You told me a while ago, you always have to pay on a Saturday afternoon, in the clubs back office so they can do their accounts and cook the clubs' books on the Saturday night after the club closes. Why not have some compensation for your loss?"

"Fucks sake Tommy! I'd thought about that!" said Billy, after a moment or two silence, "But I really want to hurt as many of those fuckers as possible, mind you, on second thoughts though, a nice little pay out won't go amiss. Me and the boys will think on it. You go and wait in me fucking car, whilst we finish up business, and I will run you to the gym."

Tommy sat in the car wondering if he should just do a runner and see Billy tomorrow, but it was no good, if Billy had it in for him he was done. What difference would a day make?

Thirty minutes later, Billy and his cronies left the pub. "You lot fuck off for the night. Me 'n' Tommy need to have a chat."

Billy drove in silence along the sea front, that joined Seaton Carew to Hartlepool. The brooding grey North Sea never long out of sight. The North Steelworks on their left hand side, spewing out smoke and steam, that seemed to choke the very air they breathed.
Eventually he parked at the Small Crafts Club, deep in Hartlepool dock land. Not a place to go, if you were a stranger to the town. Billy occasionally put some work across these doors. Mainly grafting in his scrap yard, putting the hurt on some fool, sometimes driving and occasionally, the odd 'fishing trip.'
Once Billy and Tommy entered the club, a table was cleared. Those sitting closest to it moved further away, to less favourable tables, but in this case far healthier ones. Two pints of Cameron's Strongarm were delivered to the table, with fresh beer mats and 2 pork pies. The juke box was turned up, so that no one could overhear the conversation that was to be had.
Billy commanded, and demanded, this kind of respect in the bars and pubs he used. He never took liberties. Never asked for protection money. Always paid for what he drank and if a landlord approached him for help, he would generally sort the problem out.
"Do you know why we are here Tommy" Billy asked?
"I hope it's not to go fishing Billy. I am really sorry!"
"Shut the fuck up you cunt and listen hard. What you said today was right. It makes sense and we will discuss how we do it in here. But listen the fuck up. You ever second guess me in front of anyone again and I will gut you and use you as fucking fishing bait. Do you understand?" The menace in his voice and the intensity of his stare told Tommy everything he needed to know.
"Yes Billy," he said, "and I'm sorry."

"Right now, we will have a couple of pints and a chat about how." He slapped Tommy playfully across the head and grabbed a Pork pie.
'This bloke is a class 1 psycho,' thought Tommy, but still he grinned. He had gotten away with it.
Tommy went into detail about his plan for the raid. The later they hit the nightclub the less resistance they would meet.
"The chances are, a lot of the Turk mob will have gone home or be hammered. If we go in sober and hard, subduing them quickly" said Tommy "we will be able to turn them over and be away before they have a chance to react. Balaclavas and gloves will be needed and long sleeved shirts or jackets."
"Why the fuck do we need long sleeves?" asked Billy "arms don't leave finger prints."
Tommy looked at Billy eye to eye. "Right arm hanging monkey, Liverpool football club emblem. picture of naked lady. Left arm 2 ship's anchors, mum RIP and a dragon head. I know what tattoos you have Billy and I have only known you a little while. The Turks have known you for years. If they recognise your tats, or anyone else's, we are screwed."
Billy sat back, appraising Tommy where he sat. "Fuck! You are a smart cunt aint ya? Right you are, long sleeves."
"Can't use names either Billy. To get away clean, to leave the Turks wondering, we cannot give them any clue of who we are. To be on the safe side, we can't use your regular cars. They should never see what we are driving but belts and braces Billy."
"No worries on that. I will borrow a couple of cars for the night. Reg Noble owes me a favour. He owns Stranton car sales, he'll lend us a few."

An hour or so later Billy, now 9 pints to the wind and still driving, left the club with Tommy.

"Right son, one last thing before I drop you off" he said in the car park. "I can use you. None of these wankers I keep close are half as bright, or half as handy as you. You have any ideas about how we expand, how we deal with trouble, you come to me. In a couple of years, I will have you on the top table with me, and you will be rolling in the cash. Remember though, me, nobody else, I have a temper and won't be crossed. Now jump in the fucking car, it's bastard Baltic out here."

6

Tommy got home that night and fist pumped half a dozen times before walking into the parlour, from the hallway.
"Someone looks happy." Nancy, his mum remarked. "What have you been up to?"
"Oh, nothing mum. Just had a good day, is all."
"Been running with them gangsters?" she said, her lips pursed. Stopping her knitting, she looked up at her only son.
"Mum, I've told you before. They are not gangsters. Billy has bookmakers and a scrap yard and other interests. He don't need to be a gangster."
Billys mum sighed. "You may be coming up to 16 son, but you can't pull the wool over my eyes. Yet," she said raising her knitting across her face, in a mock parody of her words.
"I really appreciate the extra money you bring into the house son. It makes a huge difference, but if you ever bring the law to my door, you will be out on your ear. Understand?"
"Yes mum and it won't happen mum. Now how about a nice ham sarnie for me supper. Plenty of pea's pudding and pepper ey?"
The words had been said, as they had been said a number of times since Tommy started work for Billy and left school. His mum, satisfied they understood each other, went into the kitchen to plate a sandwich up for him. Secretly, she was proud her son was being recognised as a face but she was the matriarch of the family and had to keep everyone, including her beer thirsty shit of a husband in line.

If ever the police knocked on her door or worse still, took Tommy away, she would be a laughing stock in the street. Unable to walk with her head held high.
Right now, she had a clean doorstep, literally and figuratively, and not even the money Tommy was bringing was worth risking that.

7

Saturday night arrived and Tommy was allowed to go with the mob. All together there were 16 of them, in 4 cars provided by Reg Noble and as planned, they arrived just before 3. They parked up around the corner from the main doors of the club. There was no such thing as CCTV in the 1960's, so as far as the Turks were concerned, they would never have a clue what vehicles were used.

Tommy had Billy make sure that all of the cars were parked facing the way they had come, for a quick getaway. If everything went to plan, they would be able to stroll out, have a fag and a piss and still drive away before a Turk would follow them down the club stairs but it was better to be prepared for the worst.

The security at the club was practically none existent, just normal mortice locks on the doors. After all, who would fuck with the Turks in their den. A tap with a sledge hammer, the guys were in and running up the stairs.

The stairs up to the club were double width and carpeted in red, which was very practical, any man fool enough to cause trouble in the club would be thrown down the stairs, after taking a pasting at the top of them. You didn't have to look too hard, to see the numerous patches of blood, on the fag burnt carpet.

It could not have been better. There were only 6 Turks in the whole of the club. Sidney the Toe, smooth Simon and Pete led their soldiers. straight into the Turks.

Only one of them, Abdul, was neither drunk or out of his head on smack. He was a fighter and put up a good show.

A slash to the belly from a razor, that required twenty eight stiches, put him out of action.

Many weeks later, once it was clear Abdul would recover from his wounds in hospital, he became known as zip belly Abdul because of the marks the stitches had left. The rest of the Turks were pretty much sitting targets, literally, as only two of the five made an effort to get to their feet, before being hammered by Billy's mob. Knuckledusters, pick axe handles and coshes worked quickly and effectively through the Turks. The count, when completed by the hospital staff, included eight broken bones, sixteen missing teeth and a finger so badly mangled it had to be removed. The Turks, either unconscious or subdued, were laid face down on the carpet and threatened with more violence if they were to move an inch.

Billy led Tommy, Irish Alf and Bobby Campbell through a set of double doors, marked VIP Room, and behind a curtain, into a corridor with a single door at the end of it. Once through the door they were in an opulent office which contained a large desk, a side table with crystal decanters and glasses, a two seater sofa with a small coffee table in front of it and two wingback chairs. In a corner, by a window, sat a safe. Also, there that night, were three bags of cash and five duffel bags full of Marijuana. Unfortunately, Omar was nowhere to be seen.

Billy had wanted to give Omar the kicking of his life, he was running on adrenalin and had hate in his heart. Secretly, Tommy was pleased Omar was not there. He liked the Turk enough to want him not to get hurt. As Omar was not in the club, the safe had to remain locked. This didn't bother Billy in the slightest. The sight of the duffel bags and their contents taking all of his attention away from the safe.

"Fuck me, Jesus fucking hell. Would you look at that. It's fucking Christmas!" shouted Billy. "Get in there, you fucker we have hit the fucking jackpot."
Ten minutes later the four cars, were heading out of Middlesbrough and onto the road to Haverton Hill, from there along the coast road to Hartlepool.
Billy had Tommy and his brother Pete in his borrowed Jag with him, along with all of the cash and drugs they had found.
He was planning Monday morning out aloud, which would involve getting every one of their dealers stashed up and pushing as hard as possible.
"We will make a fucking fortune this month," he laughed.
Pete laughed along, with Billy, as he always did. He held his older brother in awe and he was also shit scared of him. If anyone didn't laugh when Billy did, they were either in trouble already or would be, if Billy realised they didn't like his jokes. Tommy sat quiet.
"What's up with you for fucks sake," said Billy. "We just won the fucking pools and you have a fucking lemon in your mouth. It went as smooth as it fucking could, no names, long sleeves. Every fucking thing and still you have a face like a slapped arse."
"Can I tell you later?" asked Tommy.
"Tell me fucking now, for fucks sake, anything you ever have to say to me can be said in front of Pete. He's family and you are getting to be like the son I never had. So, spit it out."
'One day he tells me one thing, the next it's something else,' remembering Billy's warning from earlier in the week. 'This guy really is head fucked,' thought Tommy. However, he had been told to speak. So he did.
"Right now, the Turks have no clue who have hit them. The Geordies and that mob from York also have problems with them, so it could be one of 3 of us, or who

knows maybe even more. If all of a sudden you have a huge amount of dope hit the streets, they are gonna know it was us. They will come looking for payback Billy and you know they can raise one hell of a mob. Why not sell the dope to your contacts in Liverpool? They shift so much it won't be noticed. I know you will lose a lot of street value but you will still be quid's in and you will move it in one go, if the Turks come looking, they won't find it. The Turks are going to need to raise some capital quick, so should be keen enough to sell to you. With them desperate you can buy on the condition they close down their barber shops. If you buy from them, they will be pretty sure it wasn't us that turned them over. They will look elsewhere."

"Tommy's right" said Pete who, although was handy enough in a fight, wasn't really cut out to be a gangster and always wanted a quiet life. The idea of a potential gang war scared him shitless.

"Pete, I will fucking decide if Tommy is right or fucking wrong. Is that cunting clear?"

"Yes Billy" said Pete and went back into his shell.

"Tommy, if them fuckers want a tear up, we can give them one can we not?"

"Yeah of course we can, but look how we hit them tonight. If they hit us like that, they will give us a pasting or worse. Truth is Billy, you only have a handful of guys and me. The rest are part time hired thugs. They won't be up for a war. The Turks are slick and hard, you have to be, to hold Middlesbrough and Redcar against local mobs."

"If you sell the dope, you will have a huge amount of cash. You could buy that pub up on the Manor estate you always wanted.

The Turks might be a little suspicious about how you raised the money to buy from them when they have been cutting you short but your bookies are well established. You could get away with it. They will be looking for people who are moving blow not someone keen to buy it."

Billy said nothing for a while. Clearly the thought of a gang war, he had no hope of winning, had sunk in.

"Tell you what," he said after what seemed like an age, "come around the yard today at 11 and we will go through this again. Then we can go up town and get pissed watching the strippers. Pete, we will see you in town. Just me 'n' Tommy for this one."

It was a little before 5am when Tommy got dropped off at home by Billy. He was shattered and wired. He had never felt a rush like the one he had just had. 'Turning over the Turks was fucking ace. Stinking immigrants shouldn't be allowed in the country anyway, but turning them over and them not finding out who did it, was fucking top drawer. 'No way will I sleep,' he thought, as he crept into bed but within minutes, he was flat out.

8

Tommy got to the yard at 10:50. Billy's car was already there and that was the only one. Tommy secretly felt pleased. This was the second sit down with Billy in the last 5 days. 'Just me 'n' him,' he thought, 'no other fucker. Just me 'n' him.'
Billy had a brew on, a teapot full of strong milky tea. There must have been about half a bag of sugar in it but it was just what was needed before an afternoon on the piss. Cold bacon butties sat on Billy's desk, smothered in HP sauce, just as Billy liked them.
"Now son, come on in. Take a pew, get a buttie 'n' brew down yer neck and let's go through that plan of yours in a little more detail."
Tommy was clear and concise. If the Turks had no clue who did the job, they could not start a war. Right now the Turks were the only source of dope in the area, so Billy had to buy from them. But a trip to Liverpool, to offload what they had robbed, might also get an introduction to the Irish, who seemed to have an endless supply over on the west coast and Midlands. Selling cheap to the Liverpool guys may also create opportunities, further down the line, once trust has been established.
"Billy you make good money, great money doing what you do. Your bookies help you launder it, make it legit, without the costs, other gangs can pay to launder cash. But Hartlepool is only so big. You will only ever make so much. If you get in with the Scousers, who knows what opportunities you may get. You have the Turks cash and you will probably double that selling the blow. It's a win win Billy. No risk, maximum return and all done very quickly."
Billy sat back "You're right son. I will make a call before we leave here."

"Speaking of the money son" said Billy "your cut is more than the hired hand but less than the top table boys. You understand that?"
"Yes, of course" said Tommy.
"Well that all changes from today. None of them fuckers would even dare to speak out like you do. That's probably because they are all as thick as shit and can't think past their next fuck. You're different son. You think and act accordingly. So from now on, the share out will be me, Pete, then you, followed by the rest of them. They know it's fucking coming, so there should be no fucking surprises. But if anyone steps out of line, you deal with them, not me. OK? Brains is fine but they don't win a fight. So if you need to, you make an example, if you are badmouthed. You understand?"
"Yeah, sure Billy and thank you."
"OK. That's that. Let's get on the piss."
'OK' thought Tommy. 'Yes, fucking yes!'
"Sure Billy and thank you. I won't let you down."
"If Pete weren't blood, you would be my number 2 but that's never going to happen while he still breathes. You get me?"
"Absolutely" said Tommy, adding "I will always have both of your back's Billy." 'One way or another he thought to himself.'
'Fuck me,' thought Tommy, sitting and chewing his sandwich. Half listening to Billy go on about the birds he would fuck over the weekend. 'Top table, 3rd in line. Fucking hell, I cracked it.'

9

Later that day, the top table met at the Station Hotel. Jackie and Shirley ran the place but always shut up shop, if Billy wanted to use it for a meet. He would stuff a hand full of notes into Jackie's hand. More than they would ever earn on an afternoon and tell them to take a walk down the seafront. Have a pint in The Marine and fish and chips. If ever they came back before the guys had finished, they would just carry on to the train station and pop into town for an hour.
There was never ever any trouble in the Station. Even the most foolish piss head would never kick off in there, unless of course, they had a death wish. Everyone in the town knew this was Billy's pub of choice and no one was going to make an enemy of Billy, by disrespecting Jackie and Shirley.
Billy, Pete and Tommy were already seated when the rest of the guys wandered in at 1pm. Sidney the toe spoke first,
"Go get the beers Tommy, I'm thirsty as fuck."
"That aint his job anymore Sid" said Billy, "Tommy has been doing some work for me. Helping me plan and because of that, he now sits next to me and Pete. So if any of you fuckers want a pint. Go fucking get one."
The table went quiet. The challenge had been laid down. Now was the time to speak out, if anyone was going to. Smooth Simon, who was useful in a fight, was also exceptionally stupid. "Fuck sake Billy. He's only a snot nosed kid. What planning can this fucker do, that we can't?"
"Your fucking funeral" said Tommy with real menace in his voice. He leaned forwards across the table, "if you or any of the fuckers sat around this table have a problem

with me, let's get it sorted, in the car park. Right fucking now."

Simon looked around the table. No one was going to back him up. Now all eyes were on him.

"Fucks sake" he said. "Calm down son. If that's how Billy wants it. That's how it will be."

"Good" said Tommy "and one more thing and this is for you all. I aint your fucking son. I'm Tommy and never ask me to do anything, you can do yourselves. Only Billy and Pete do that. Clear?"

The table mumbled their responses. Clearly not happy, but like most people who work in a fixed hierarchy, once the pecking order was established, they would comply.

"Now, the bar's there. You want a beer, go fucking get one" said Tommy, finishing the conversation.

Tommy saw a look of pure hatred pass across Simon's face. 'I'm going to have to watch this one,' he thought.

"Good," said Billy, "that's that sorted. Now whilst you cock suckers have all been doing fuck all, wasting your time, us three have decided what we do next. I placed a call, this morning to a face I know in Liverpool.

Tomorrow, we take a road trip to Birkenhead. Us three in the lead car, you lot follow in Sidney's and Alf's cars. We are taking the blow with us and will be selling to the mob over there. We won't get street value obviously, but we will get quick cash and the Turks will have no idea who hit them, as we won't be selling their shit. Speaking of that, make sure the lads we took know to keep this under wraps. If any crap comes back to this door whoever opened his mouth will be with the fishes.

Bobby and Simon, you two got them together so you can deliver the message personally to each one of them, and make sure you fucking do!

Now, we got almost £6000 off those greasy bastards Saturday night. You 4 get £500 each, the lads you brought £50 and the rest goes into the business. Any questions?"

"What about the money for the blow?" asked Bobby, "will you be divvying that up?"

"No. That goes to the business. We could do with another bookies in Stockton and that will sort it," said Billy. "If all goes to plan, you will each get a lump up in your weeklies, once it is established and turning over. Right, meet in the Owton Lodge car park, tomorrow at 6am. Now fuck off. We got stuff to talk about. If you want a beer tonight, come around the scrap yard no benders tonight. The mob over there, need to see serious gangsters, not pissed up Northern cunts."

Quietly and quickly, the table and the bar emptied.

"You see how it works Tommy?" said Billy, as the door closed behind Smooth Simon, the last to leave. "Those cunts must know we got a load more than £6k but they don't have the balls to challenge me. If they went it alone, they would be working in the Steel Works for peanuts within weeks. Or if I had a mind to it, they would be swimming with the fishes.

Here this is yours. There's £3000 there. Don't fucking lose it and don't buy nothing too flash."

The meeting at Liverpool the next day went off without any drama, they met at a transport café just outside of Birkenhead. Billy was a Scouser. He knew some of the lads he was dealing with. There was a quick check of the product Billy was moving and then the deal was done. Whilst the money they were paid for the blow was well below retail, it was cash and it meant they were clean with the Turks.

10

'£3000,' thought Tommy to himself, as he shifted on the ground. The dark blankets he had brought with him keeping most of the damp off his aching bones.
'Wouldn't get me a suit now, but fuck, I thought I had won the pools.'
Tommy remembered running home that day, the wad of money stuffed into a haversack on his back. He rarely had time for the gym those days. Not enough to keep boxing, for sure, but he ran regularly and did spar at least twice per week.
He was a natural athlete. He could pretty much eat and drink what he wanted and remain toned and muscular. A run like this was like free exercise for him. On impulse he veered off Brenda Rd and followed Belle Vue Way into town, making short time of the 2 miles or so, to the towns biggest department store, Binns. Ten minutes later he had purchased a 32" Pye TV. The display model had a price of £85 on it, but his old school mate Mark Bowman said, he could do one that afternoon for £50 cash. Deal done. Tommy then wandered through the town to Tanners estate agents on York Road. Gary Tanners was 2 years older than Tommy but they had boxed together for years and were best mates. Tommy took Gary for a pint in the Park Hotel and told him what he was looking for.
Eight weeks later, Tommy was the proud owner of a two bed terraced house in Dent Street, and a three bedroom in Calcutta Grove. It had taken the balance of the cash and another £700 he had in savings but he owned two houses. Not only that, Gary had tenants in both, paying a total of £42 a week. Not bad for a lad only just sixteen, he thought to himself.

Gary had set up a holding company for Tommy, so that no one knew it was him that owned the properties. He also knew a solicitor that would cut through the red tape of someone as young as Tommy buying properties. He charged a little more but was good and trustworthy and that's all that mattered to Tommy.

Tommy had spent quite a bit of time with Gary Tanners over the next couple of weeks. Some of it was to complete the legal side of the property purchase and some to plan further investments. Gary was sound, Tommy trusted him and although he never spoke of what he did for Billy, they did speak of further investment opportunities.

Along with the residential side of Tanners business there was a commercial side, very often they became involved with town planners. Gary would keep Tommy in the loop if there was ever money to be made. Gary and Tommy were of the same mind, they both wanted to make money, as much as they could, with as much of that as possible being legitimate, even if the source of the funds were less so.

Gary had two brothers. His dad's estate agent business was barely supporting the family now. There was no way it would support three families, once the brothers were married. The plan was quite simple. Tommy would provide the capital, Gary would provide the insider knowledge and when the time was right, they would set up a joint venture.

As Tommy's turned seventeen his retainer with Billy was now £100 per week. He gave his Mam £15, saved £50 and spent the rest on clothes, booze and most recently a year old Ford Cortina mark 2 1600E. He had passed his test and wanted some 'top wheels.' 'Life was good,' he thought to himself 'but not good enough.' He wanted more, his life felt a little mundane and he had begun to resent being told what to do by Billy all of the time. True he was earning more than he could doing anything else. The hours he actually worked were next to nowt. But he knew he could do much better than Billy if he were in charge, the problem was how?

Before Tommy knew it, he was 18 years old. Billy and the boys took him out and they had a right royal piss up to celebrate. Tommy, like Billy, had no intentions of settling down with a bird. His reputation around town, as a face, meant there was a queue of women keen to bed Tommy, which suited him just fine. There were one or two women that he knew, would do almost anything he asked in the sack but they were proper slappers. He really enjoyed the chase and once he had bedded a woman, he just lost interest.

Tommy now had three houses all paid for, no mortgages, bringing him in £68 per week. With the money he was earning from Billy, he was doing better than anyone he knew and, other than Gary, better than anyone else knew he was doing. Billy and the crew had no idea that Tommy was investing and it would stay that way. If it all went pear shaped with the gang, he had enough coming in to see him by until better, more lucrative opportunities came his way. He thirsted for power and for sure, wealth was the best way to get it. He still lived at home, trained hard when he could and continued to work closely with Billy.

Billy was becoming a problem though. He had started to use drugs heavily and was nearly always smashed. He was leaving the running of the gang to Pete and Tommy but still taking a huge cut of the money that came in from the bookies, drug sales and now a pub too.

Every Saturday, Tommy would drive over to the Turks with a bag full of cash and drive back with 2 or 3 bags of gear, to be distributed out to their network of pushers.

He was also responsible for the bookies. Dropping in, unannounced, checking paid out betting slips for anomalies and generally keeping the managers on their toes.

He bounced at the pub, if it were needed, and all of the time Billy was as high as a fucking kite. Pete was a nice guy but was not cut out for this life. So Billy pretty much came to Tommy every time he had an issue.

"Something has to fucking change" Tommy said to Gary Tanners one night, "these two are running me ragged."

11

Over the months, Tommy had begrudgingly come to respect the Turks and Omar. Especially the way they ran their business, clean, efficient and, if needs be, ruthlessly. Their organisation was pretty much perfect, with each man in it understanding his role and where he sat within the organisation, which impressed Tommy no end. Their transactions were slick and professional. If you showed the right amount of respect, paid when you should, as much as you should, transactions with the Turks were pretty much problem free.
Omar who was head of the gang started taking tea with Tommy, when he arrived to exchange cash for drugs. This was another job that had become exclusively Tommy's.
At first, Tommy resented spending the extra time in Middlesbrough. It was Saturday after all. He wanted to get a frame or 2 of snooker in before hitting the town, but Omar was curiously interesting. He took an interest in Tommy, his family and his role within Billy's organisation. He also told Tommy how he ran his empire, how he structured his team, how he rewarded, how he punished. He told Tommy that every man who worked for him was of Turkish origins but if Tommy ever wanted work put his way, Omar would welcome him with open arms.
"I have many eyes" he told Tommy, "I see everything in Hartlepool. You are the man now, the brothers are no force without you. One a drug user, one a coward. You have brains Tommy. Use them."
Privately Tommy was pleased that Omar held him in such regard but there was no way he could take a job with the Turks. Not in a million years.
He has thought long and hard about setting up himself but Billy still had enough clout in Hartlepool. Not only

with thugs, but with bent coppers too. That, Tommy knew, he would be shut down and buried within weeks, if he were to try to go alone.

One Saturday, just weeks before Tommy would turn 19, he sat having Turkish tea with Omar in his office. The tea was always served black and sweet, not to Tommy's taste but he always drained his cup out of respect.

"Now Tommy" said Omar "we have a problem. Tell me. Can you count?"

"Yeah of course" said Tommy.

"Ok. The money you brought today is on that table, bring it over" Tommy did and was asked to count the bundles. He found seventeen bundles of £500 in mixed notes.

"£8500 Omar, as agreed," said Tommy.

"Good. Now count a bundle" insisted Omar. Tommy did. He started a little nervous. 'There must be a reason for this' he thought, and finished counting the bundle, in a cold sweat. It was £10 short.

"Any bundle you choose Tommy" said Omar "all £10 short. Who gives you the money?"

"Billy does," said Tommy.

"And Billy knows what we do to people who rob us" asked Omar.

"Yes" said Tommy.

"So" said Omar "he is prepared to sacrifice you for £170 a week. This is a problem, Tommy. Yes?"

"Yes" said Tommy.

"OK" said Omar, "I like you, Tommy. You are a good guy, a thinking man. Do you think you can resolve this problem to my satisfaction Tommy? To my total satisfaction?"

The message was clear. Tommy must kill Billy. Repay the debt, with a gift of respect added or Tommy would be a target himself.

"Yes, Omar I will deal with this by the time I visit next Saturday."
"Perfect. Shall we have another cup of tea?"
Omar spent the rest of his time with Tommy as if the conversation, they had just finished, had never happened.
The drive back to Hartlepool was a long one for Tommy. He had no problem giving a guy a good slapping. Indeed, he would even break bones but to kill a man? A man, he once considered a friend, was going to be hard. It had to be done right too. If ever he was suspected, of turning on his boss, there would be no sanctuary for him in the country, never mind the town!
Billy was now, pretty much, living in the scrapyard office. It was a portacabin. No windows, cold and inhospitable. He ventured out, to go on benders, with the boys. Occasionally, to attend to business. For the most part, he sat in the office, smoking Opium and getting shitfaced. Like most druggies his personal hygiene had disappeared and he was more and more paranoid.
He had a couple of pot head bitches, that would come over to the yard. Do for Billy whatever he wanted and leave with a purse full of blow. Billy was a wreck, a disgrace, but he was still ruthless. Nobody would cross him. Unless someone was summoned, only Pete and Tommy were allowed to visit the yard.
'He has it coming,' thought Tommy 'I just wish it didn't have to be me' He had been wronged as much as Omar. So, despite the feelings of guilt, he would carry out the task himself. It was a matter of pride. Billy had been prepared to sacrifice him, for a few quid skimmed off the top. Tommy had to be the one that righted the wrong.

12

Tommy decided to act on Tuesday night. He made sure he was seen around town that night, drinking in some of the trendier bars which he had begun to frequent. Moving from bar to bar, it was difficult for anyone to say how much he had to drink, but the assumption would have been a lot. He had, in fact, had very little. He left town as the pubs closed and got a taxi home. Chatting to the driver and tipping him a fiver, just to make sure the driver remembered collecting and dropping him.
Around 2am, he arrived at the scrapyard, on foot. It was a forty minute run from his mum's house. His car not moving from in front of the house. He entered the yard using his keys. Instead of walking to the office, he took a short detour, collecting a set of bolt cutters that he had left out the previous afternoon. He then relocked the padlock, before cutting it, using the bolt cutters. After wiping these and the padlock down, he put the bolt cutters back into the workshop and left the padlock on the floor by the gate.
As Tommy had expected, Billy was out of it, asleep on an old couch. A string of saliva falling from his lips, almost to the floor. Tommy looked down on Billy. He felt a moment of pity and remorse. What had become of the man he once feared and respected? He was fat, he stunk and it looked like he had pissed himself. He was lying in his own filth, all but unconscious.
Billy had become more and more erratic when dealing with his business. Twice recently, Tommy had ignored orders to beat someone, because Billy had imagined a slight. Telling Billy it had been dealt with, whilst tipping off the potential victim, to lay low for a week or so.
"Billy what happened to you?" he whispered, then hit him hard across the head with a leather cosh.

Billy grunted and slipped from the couch to the floor. Tommy then had to strip his former boss naked, gritting his teeth and breathing through his mouth. He completed the task. Lifting an unconscious man is not easy, Billy weighed in about fifteen stone and it took Tommy some time to get him onto, and tied into, his office chair. Tommy gagged him, just in case he awoke. Then using Billy's keys, that he always left in his top drawer he opened the floor safe that was hidden under an old rug. It was crammed with money and gold sovereigns, that Billy had always had a fondness for.

"Always have gold," he said to Tommy one day, "it's the best currency in the world."

The gold and money safely bagged up by the door, Tommy turned to the inevitable task in front of him. He stripped naked, took a cut throat razor and did just that. Grabbing Billy by the hair and cutting his throat.

Tommy had not imagined that Billy's blood would pump out as far and as fiercely as it did. He was stood behind Billy, so got little on himself. Very quickly Tommy sliced Billy's cheeks, his arms and legs, all wounds bleeding enough so that no one would realise they were done after the fatal wound but before Billy was dead.

He took his fingers and twisted them out of their sockets. Torturing a dead man was disgusting but Tommy saw it as a mercy. This had to look right. It had to be done, so it was better to do it to a Billy who was dead than alive.

It took Billy less than 2 minutes to stop gurgling and take his last desperate breath. A sad, almost melancholy rattle in his throat, signalling the end of Billy the Scouse. Thankfully for Tommy, he did not wake up, although Tommy was ready to look him in the eyes if he did. The offices had a toilet and sink. Billy rinsed his arms and chest in the sink and left the tap running to clean it out as he dressed. He gathered the bag of money and gold

and left. Leaving the yard gate pushed to, but not closed. He had worn gloves from before he entered the portacabin until after he left. There was very little forensic science back in the day and no DNA. If there were no witnesses and no finger prints you got away clean. Unless, of course, the coppers fitted you up. Tommy knew that the next day or 2 would be critical. If he got past those, he would probably be ok. He was confident he had planned well and not been seen.
On the way home Tommy made a slight detour to an abandoned heavy engineering company on Brenda Road. There he hid the bag, under a piece of old asbestos roofing, in a ditch that ran between the old factory and scrubland. Not ideal but the best he could do. Should the cops decide to search all of Billy's known associates, they would find nothing in his house. Finally, when he got home, he bagged up all of the clothes and the running shoes he had been wearing, before going to sleep for 2 hours.

13

Pete was normally first to the yard in the morning, arriving around 7am. Tommy normally dropped in anywhere from 8 to 9, depending on what collections and drops he did in the morning, to the gang's pushers. Fortunately, Wednesday was a quiet morning. So, Tommy only had a few calls to make, and 1 bag of clothes to burn, at his uncle's allotment at the bottom of Bolton Grove.

When he arrived at the yard a little after 8, Pete was pacing up and down outside the office. Drawing heavily and constantly on a fag, that glowed red as if in protest.

"Where the fuck have you been?" he yelled at Tommy.
"Fucking hell Pete. You never get your leg over last night? What the fuck is wrong?" he replied.
"Fucking hell, what's fucking wrong? Have a look in the office. That's what's fucking wrong! We are fucking screwed Tommy." Tommy looking puzzled walked into the office and ran back out, retching for good effect.
"Fuck Pete! What the fuck happened?"
"I don't fucking know! He was like that when I got here."
"Have you called the old bill?" Tommy asked.
"No, I didn't know what to fucking do."
"OK I will call them now. Fucking hell, I'm going to have to go back in there to use the phone. I don't suppose you would like to?" Tommy asked Pete.
"Fuck off! He's my fucking brother. I can't look at him like that."

So, Tommy braved the office, one more time, to dial 999 and explain to the police what would be waiting for them at the yard.

He then ran out and slapped Pete's face. Not hard but hard enough, to make him focus.

"The bizzies are going to be all over this," he said, "the safe has been turned over. We have 5 minutes to get our story straight, so listen up. Billy was a business man, we ran errands for him and looked after some of his bookies. Is that clear? Say nothing fucking else. They have nothing on us, so say fuck all, especially about the drugs and the contents of the safe. It doesn't matter if the cop is on the books or not, say nothing, trust no one ok? Pete! Fucking focus, are you listening?"
"Yeah, sorry Tommy. I won't say a thing."
"Right the coppers will be here soon, as will the 2 guys who work here. You found him at 7, you were so distraught you didn't think straight, which is why I called it in just after eight. OK?"
"Yeah Tommy. OK."
With that the clanging of a police bell could be heard and a Ford Prefect came tearing into the yard, to start what would be a very long fucking day.
Fortunately for Tommy, one of the two officers who arrived was Derek Hogan. Tommy had helped him out once, when his daughter got mixed up, with a serial woman beater. Tommy had given the guy a hiding that Derek couldn't, and warned him off his daughter. Derek had told Tommy that day that he owed him one. Not that covering for a murder would have been what he meant but Tommy was still grateful to see Derek step out of the panda car.
"Now then Tommy," said Derek, "what's going on?"
"In the office" Tommy replied, "and it aint pretty Derek."
Derek wandered off and less than a minute later, he was back.
"OK guys, you are going to have to stay here till the tec's arrive, to interview you." He looked directly at Pete, "I am sorry for your loss" he said, showing the respect that coppers did back in the day, especially coppers that took

45

the odd favour. "We will do everything to catch who did this for you Pete. Do you have any ideas?"

"Not really Derek," replied Pete. "Billy didn't venture out too much recently, he had been a little unwell of late."

'Unwell,' thought Tommy to himself, ' that's one way of putting it.'

Tommy saw Derek roll his eyes. Everyone who knew Billy, knew he was on a downwards spiral.

Back then, the police an uneasy existence with criminals. Rarely trying too hard to investigate gang on gang crime but coming down heavy on any activity that made the papers or involved innocent members of the public.

Billy had four coppers on the pay roll, two sergeants and two detectives. Most big time criminals did. It didn't make them above the law but it helped.

It was one of these detectives that arrived next. Sid O'Donnell was as lazy a copper anyone had seen, and as bent as any copper outside of London. After a quick view of the body, he took Pete to one side, firstly asking if he would still get his wedge at the end of the month and then if Pete had any idea who did it? Finally, telling Pete he was sorry for his loss. He quickly established the bones of Pete's story, corroborated them with Tommy and then asked Tommy who he thought might have done it. Tommy shrugged his shoulders.

"No idea Sid" he said, "I know Billy had his enemies but fuck, all that blood!" Concentrating on what he had seen, rather than the question Sid had asked. Sid was happy enough with the answer but persisted.

"No ideas at all Tommy?" he asked hopefully."

"None Sid but whoever did it, I don't want to fucking cross them, for sure."

"That's a message Tommy" said Sid, "you must have crossed someone big. The Turks maybe or the Petersons, up at Newcastle."

"No idea" replied Tommy, looking the copper in his face, "all I do is run the bookies and the pub."

"What about the safe?" asked the copper, "how much was in there?"

"No idea Sid. Float for the yard, maybe? Some spare cash? Not really sure. Never knew it was there until I saw it open this morning, when I went in the office to call you lot."

Sid smiled. The less Tommy and Pete told him, the less he had to go on, the quicker he could close the case as unresolved. If luck went his way, it would not interrupt the income from Pete, that he hoped would continue now he was in charge and not Billy.

"Remember everything you have told me Tommy. If anyone else asks you, exactly the same answers buddy, no surprises now" was Sid's parting message.

Tommy knew Sid would be more interested in finding the contents of the safe, rather than the identity of the killer of Billy. 'Not only is he useless as a copper but fuck, he is greedy too,' thought Tommy.

The rest of the day for Pete and Tommy was much the same. Different people, same questions, and the same answers.

A little before 6pm, Tommy and Pete were allowed to leave the yard. They went straight to the Station Hotel, where the rest of the top table guys were gathered in the back snug. A chair in front of the door, warning off casual drinkers.

As Tommy and Pete walked in, the room erupted in questions. Everyone wanting to know what had happened and what would happen next. News carried quickly in Hartlepool. The yard men, having been sent

home by the coppers, had called on Sidney one toe, telling him something was going down at the yard. He had soon rounded up the rest of the gang.
"Shut the fuck up," said Tommy. "Shut up, the fucking lot of yer."
Quickly, he explained to everyone, what Pete had found that morning. Running through the way Billy had died and that the safe was empty. Tommy was explicit, with what he had saw that morning, the tortured body of Billy. He wanted the gang scared and easy to manipulate.
"The Bizzies think it was a hit. A professional one and it fucking looked like it was too. So, who has leaked what, and to who, we need to know and quickly. Tomorrow, Smooth Simon will come with me to do the drops and collections. We need to double up wherever we can, go out in pairs. Be careful in case this aint done. If you get so much as an itch, be on your toes, who knows if this stops with Billy.
Everyone in the town will know Billy is dead by now, so we need to act quickly and hard. Make sure no one takes liberties with us.
Sid and Alf, you visit every pusher we have that me and Simon won't see tomorrow and remind them who pays their bills and who supplies them. We can't have anyone taking liberties. The Turks will want paying Saturday, come what may.
Bobby, visit every bookies. Tell the managers what has happened. It's business as usual and if anyone of them has an idea about putting a hand in the till, tell them we will cut the fucker off.
Pete, I guess you will need to take care of the funeral arrangements, with the COOP. We will all meet up with you tomorrow night, back here at six sharp. Now, listen up everyone, keep on your toes. This looked like a pro hit. If it was, they may be coming back, for one or all of

us. Remember, ears to the ground. We need to know who did this and why?"

"Come on Pete" said Tommy, "I will get you home. You have a busy day tomorrow."

Tommy drove Pete back into town, to drop him at his house in Flaxton Street. As they drove through Burn Valley, Pete said "It was the Turks Tommy. They did it."

"How the fuck do you know that?" Tommy asked.

"Billy was shorting their money. He told me last week. Laughed like fuck about it. Said the stupid fuckers couldn't count shit anyway!"

Tommy slammed the anchors on and brought the car to a halt.

"He was shorting the fucking Turks and sending me in there with the cash alone? The fucking cunt! That could be me all cut up. Why the fuck didn't you tell me Pete?"

"I wanted to" Pete replied meekly, "but you know what Billy's like. He would've beat the shit out of me."

"I should fucking do the same, you cunt," said Tommy. "Well, I tell you what. You will do the drop Saturday. No way am I going over there."

"Tommy please, I can't. You know I am no good at this sort of thing. All I want is a quiet life, you know that."

Tommy sat brooding, clenching his huge hands, breathing noisily through his nose. After a minute, his body relaxed. "Sorry Pete. That was just a shock, you know. Fuck sake! Why would he do that? I could have been carved up, every Saturday, because of what he done. OK, I will take care of the Turks on Saturday. If I survive that, we will talk."

The conversation finished, Tommy dropped Pete off and headed home. He was now absolutely sure that Pete would do whatever he was told, if it was delivered the right way. There was no way Pete would ever suspect Tommy. He was too busy being grateful that Tommy was picking up the shitty end of the stick, by visiting the Turks.

14

Things went relatively smoothly over the next few days. No one stepped out of line, other than one dealer, who got on his toes with his stash and the cash he had taken on the gang's behalf.

He was quickly caught and given the beating of his life. Put in the boot of Sidney the toe's car and driven around to every other dealer they had, as an example of what would happen should they try to take liberties. He was kicked out of his house and a new dealer moved in. Times were tough in Hartlepool and there was always a queue of willing men, to do whatever they could to earn a wage.

On Thursday evening, Tommy and Gary Tanners collected the bag of cash and gold that Tommy had stashed in the early hours of Wednesday morning and went back to Gary's father's shop, to count it.

"Not sure I have seen this much cash before" said Gary "there's nearly £22k there, without the gold coins. They must be worth £15K too!"

"Right," said Tommy "you need to keep this safe. There is still a chance the bizzies could pop round mine and roll it over. We will get together on Sunday and sort out what we are doing with it. This is our chance, Gary. Opportunities don't come around like this often, we need to make sure we take this one."

On Saturday, Tommy arrived at the Turks as normal, for his 1pm drop and collection.

"Tommy" said Omar grabbing him by his arms and kissing each cheek, as a sign of respect, "you have done well. I am told the Police have stopped asking questions. The case will be closed next week."

Omar knew more than Tommy and Pete did. As ever when Omar told Tommy something he did not know, he was impressed by how well the Turks operated.

"I have had a word with the lead detective. He is clear that he will not resolve this case. It will be put down to gang on gang. I have told him not to look in my direction. Come, now to business, do you have everything I expect?" asked Omar, looking pointedly at the suitcase Tommy was carrying.

"No" said Tommy

"No?" Omar repeated. "I thought I had made myself clear. Maybe you disrespect me, Tommy?"

"Of course not Omar, never, you have taught me so much. Please hear me out."

Tommy began to tell Omar of his plans. "There will come a time Omar, when you will push hard into Hartlepool. Blood may be spilled, maybe even lives lost. I want to avoid that.

What I have brought you is £8500 and a book. In the book is the name and address of every pusher we have. I am buying next week's drugs for them, for you.

As of tomorrow, you own every pusher we have in Hartlepool, Billingham and Blackhall."

"This is more than I could have expected Tommy. Why do you do this?"

"Because when I leave here, I will visit Pete and tell him that you have took the money. Not given us the drugs and that you now control the pushers. I will tell him, that he will be contacted with an offer, for the bookies and the pub. It will be a sensible offer, to the brother of a man that had crossed you, Omar. An offer that will only be made once, in an effort to avoid further blood loss. That offer will be made by a solicitor, on behalf of a company that I own. I will be buying the bookies and the pub. Every bookies will allow one of your men in to sell drugs. They will need to be respectable and discreet. The pub will be off limits. I want a respectable pub, no drugs. Should you need me to, I will launder cash for you, through the bookies. I will sort out local issues for you if needed and introduce you to the right policemen, if there are any you don't own. I buy property Omar. Within 5 to 8 weeks, I will have 4 shops, on the biggest estates in Hartlepool.

If you choose to, you can rent these shops from me. You could have barbers pushing, as you did before. It worked well for you. If you rent from me, there will be no inspections, no hassle from landlords. I will take care of all low level chatter, that you might get from residents or the council. The rent will be no more than 10% above market, with my guarantee of goodwill. This is much more than you expected when I arrived this afternoon. I hope that you find my plan acceptable?"

"And if I don't" said Omar, "what then Tommy?"

"Well then, I will need to pop down to my car and get the other £5k I have for you. Collect my drugs and be on my way."

Omar looked hard at Tommy for a second, then laughed, clasping Tommy by the arms. He looked at him.

"You truly are a thinker, Tommy. It is a good deal, I think. I will need you to visit the pushers, with my guys tomorrow, so they understand who they work for now."

"Of course, Omar, no problems there."

"Tell me Tommy. Are you going straight?"

"Not straight Omar, but a good house. A good life style is easier for a businessman, than it is for a crook. Anyone looking at me, will see a successful man, a role model. I enjoy my life Omar, and will always look at any opportunity that comes my way, but I will minimise risk. You, Omar, have a great team around you. A trustworthy team. I have fools and bullies. Fools land people in jail"

he smiled at Omar, "and I am way too pretty for jail. I have learnt a lot from you Omar, drugs are not my path, I will find another way."
Omar laughed. "Maybe one-day Tommy, you will be teaching me. One more thing Tommy. What is ours is ours. Make sure you do not look to our businesses with anything, other than respect."
"Absolutely" came the reply "now, do we take something stronger than tea, to celebrate?"
Tommy left Omar around 6pm and drove straight to the scrapyard, where Pete sat in the dark waiting. Just a single desk lamp lighting the dingy office. It stunk of bleach and most of the furniture had been removed.
"How did it go Tommy? Everything all right?"
"No Pete it's not."
Tommy told Pete what he had planned to tell him, then they set out to find the rest of the gang. Saturday night always started in the Snooker club, in Stranton, and this Saturday was no exception. Within 20 minutes, everyone was back at the office, in the yard.
"Right boys," said Tommy. "This is what is happening. As of tomorrow, the pushers belong to the Turks every fucking one of them. For the last month Billy had been short changing them. Pete told me this last Thursday and Omar confirmed it today. It must have been the Turks that turned Billy over."
"Fuck em," said Irish Alf. "If they want a war, we give them a war. They don't just fucking walk in and take our patch."
"Alf," said Tommy. "I had to sit there and listen as Omar listed my address, your address, everyone's address here. Your mums address, in Ireland, for fucks sake. On and on, they must have had eyes on us for weeks.
If you, and I say you because I will have no part of it, if you go up against them, they will kill you. These boys

aint fucking around. We have no money, no gear, and no hope. They must have 50 guys in Middlesbrough alone and I don't know where one of them lives. Do you? We will be sitting fucking ducks. But that's only the start of it. They will be buying the bookies too."
Silence filled the office. Everyone looked to Pete. He coughed.
"They said they will make an offer that I can't refuse, and I won't be refusing it. You guys know me and I am not Billy. If he was still here and if he was in his prime, not how he was the last year or so, we might have had a chance but he's gone. There are 5 of us 6, including Tommy, we have no chance. Our games up. I will sort out Billy's funeral, sell up to the Turks and head back to Tranmere, for a quiet life."
"It's not all bad news," said Tommy. If you want to work for the Turks, they will take you on for a few months, whilst they get established but that's it guys. Our days are over."
Smooth Simon spoke next "You sure there's nothing we can do Tommy. You're the brains in the room. Is there nothing?"
"Not a thing buddy. If we had the money from the safe, we maybe would have stood a chance but that's gone too. It was good while it lasted but it's done."
Sidney the toe spoke up next. "Fuck it, I'm off too. My brother-in-law has a pub in Portsmouth. He said he would teach me the ropes and put me in as a manager of another one, if ever I wanted to. Our Julie is always harping on about it, so I guess I will be off soon."
Tommy pulled a bottle of whisky out of Billy's desk, took a swig and passed it to Pete.
"To Billy" he said. Pete took a swig and passed it on, each man toasting Billy. It did a lap and a half before the bottle was empty.

"Pete, if you are off, what do you want for the yard?" asked Tommy.
 "£5k and its yours," came the reply.
"£3K it is then," said Tommy.
Pete sighed, "yeah why the fuck not?"

15

Billy was buried,10 days later, on a miserable Tuesday afternoon. Pete, Tommy, smooth Simon, Bobby Campbell and Irish Alf were at the graveside. Sidney the toe had already left town. A few guys, that had done the odd bit of work for Billy, also turned up but the turnout was poor. Later in the Shades, on Church Street, where everyone had gone for the wake, Pete and Tommy sat talking.
"I can't believe it Tommy. I thought the Church would've been full."
Tommy reached out and grabbed Pete's shoulder.
"There's a new sheriff in town now Pete. People don't want to upset the Turks and truth be known, a lot of people had lost respect for Billy once he got too dependent on the drugs. It's easier for people to stay away. This way they show respect to the Turks, respect and fear.
The people that mattered are here. You will always be my friend, Pete, but our old life died with Billy. Truth is, it was dying once he hit the drugs. Remember him as he was a few years ago and enjoy today the best you can. Billy taught me a lot. I will always be grateful for that, but the biggest lesson Pete was to stay off the drugs. Remember that for the rest of your life pal."
Tommy had no regrets about what had transpired. He had proved himself, not only to Omar, which was very important but to himself. He had taken a man's life. He had planned it, executed it and here he was, richer and wiser.
The next day, Pete and Tommy met up again, at Tommy's scrap yard.
 "Have the Turks been in touch?" asked Tommy.

"Yeah. They offered £18K for the bookies. They fucking well make that in less than 6 months, the robbing bastards."
"Well with the £3K I have given you and the money you will get from selling your house, you will be fine for years. Pete let's face it; it could have been a lot fucking worse."
"What about you Tommy? What will you do?"
"Well, I have the yard, that makes about £2.5k a year, without trying. If I work hard at that, I am sure I can make enough to get by. After that, fuck knows but I will sort something out. I aint going to be a grease monkey all me life that's for sure."

16

Three months later, Glentower holdings purchased the leases, and goodwill, of the bookmaker shops. Pete had already left town, Irish Alf had too, going back to Belfast. "There aint no cunting Turks there" he said, the last time Tommy saw him.
Tommy and Gary Tanners set up a small estate agency in town. Gary's dad had been a little disappointed that his son had gone it alone, but everyone in the family saw sense in what was happening, and who knows if they worked together, they might be able to squeeze a couple of competitors out of business.
There was still £18K, of the £37k Tommy had lifted from Billy's safe, left. Tommy and Gary spent that on land that skirted the Fens estate and Clavering. They knew more houses would be coming to the town, people wanted to live away from the rundown town centre and older estates like the Wager, the town centre and Old Town. Their business arrangement was a simple one, 66% Tommy, 34% Gary. After all, Tommy had fronted the money.
Gary was responsible for the day to day running of their portfolio, keeping Tommy aware of any opportunities or issues.
The bookies were now all grossing more, since Tommy had taken over, and taken an interest. Three managers had been sacked for skimming, one of which, Barry Small, had taken a real pasting and told to leave town, when the level of his activity had become clear. Word soon got around, that Tommy was running the bookies for the Turks and that suited Tommy just fine. He was a hard man, one of the toughest in the town, but the Turks were a gang and whilst some may think about taking Tommy on, no one was silly enough to take on the

"Yeah. They offered £18K for the bookies. They fucking well make that in less than 6 months, the robbing bastards."

"Well with the £3K I have given you and the money you will get from selling your house, you will be fine for years. Pete let's face it; it could have been a lot fucking worse."

"What about you Tommy? What will you do?"

"Well, I have the yard, that makes about £2.5k a year, without trying. If I work hard at that, I am sure I can make enough to get by. After that, fuck knows but I will sort something out. I aint going to be a grease monkey all me life that's for sure."

16

Three months later, Glentower holdings purchased the leases, and goodwill, of the bookmaker shops. Pete had already left town, Irish Alf had too, going back to Belfast.
"There aint no cunting Turks there" he said, the last time Tommy saw him.

Tommy and Gary Tanners set up a small estate agency in town. Gary's dad had been a little disappointed that his son had gone it alone, but everyone in the family saw sense in what was happening, and who knows if they worked together, they might be able to squeeze a couple of competitors out of business.

There was still £18K, of the £37k Tommy had lifted from Billy's safe, left. Tommy and Gary spent that on land that skirted the Fens estate and Clavering. They knew more houses would be coming to the town, people wanted to live away from the rundown town centre and older estates like the Wager, the town centre and Old Town. Their business arrangement was a simple one, 66% Tommy, 34% Gary. After all, Tommy had fronted the money.

Gary was responsible for the day to day running of their portfolio, keeping Tommy aware of any opportunities or issues.

The bookies were now all grossing more, since Tommy had taken over, and taken an interest. Three managers had been sacked for skimming, one of which, Barry Small, had taken a real pasting and told to leave town, when the level of his activity had become clear. Word soon got around, that Tommy was running the bookies for the Turks and that suited Tommy just fine. He was a hard man, one of the toughest in the town, but the Turks were a gang and whilst some may think about taking Tommy on, no one was silly enough to take on the

Turks. There were those who thought that Tommy had sold out, working for the Turks but none were stupid enough to voice their thoughts in public.

17

Omar and Tommy took tea once a week, they alternated between Middlesbrough and Hartlepool. Omar always took a keen interest in what Tommy was doing with his businesses, especially the purchase of land and how Gary had structured the holding company for them both. He confirmed that he was happy with the payments for the 3 shops, he rented from Tommy and on occasion, they played a game of draughts.

It was Christmas 1975, when Omar asked Tommy if he would do him a great favour and crush a car for him. He offered to pay for the service which Tommy, as expected, declined.

The following day, an hour after everyone had left for the night, the car entered the Yard. One man got out and watched, as Tommy picked the car up with a grab crane before dropping it into the compactor. Fifteen minutes later, another bundle of scrap was added to the piles in Tommy's yard. The next collection of scrap was booked for 3rd January and that would be that.

Tommy said a short prayer for the poor soul that must have been in the boot of the car, but business is business, and goodwill with Omar was priceless.

18

Flexing his fingers, Tommy checked his Rolex, coming up to 5 o'clock. 'I fucking hope he shits the bed.' thought Tommy. 'I am fucking freezing. I don't fancy another 2 hours under this bush.' It was still dark, as it would be at 6.30 am, when John Jameson should walk around the corner to his garage. Tommy knew he had arrived way earlier than he could have done but this was his way. Be safe, reduce every possible eventuality, narrow every parameter reduce every risk as far as possible and everything should go well.

19

It was July 1979, just after Tommy's 29th birthday. Business was good and by reinvesting most of the income Glentower Holdings had accrued, their property portfolio included 28 houses, 17 retail units including 9 bookmakers, and 4 video shops, that were for a few years anyway, absolute goldmines.

Tommy and Gary worked well together. Always looking for opportunities to advance themselves, to become wealthier and more legitimate. They had opened a loans business, offering all the domestic appliances that so many people rented, back in the day. Along with personal loans, some of which were never entered into the company accounts. Whilst this was time consuming, it was also very lucrative. Small loans, with higher than high street bank interest rates, kept the poor in towns like Hartlepool going. There was no shame in taking a loan, just shame in not being able to pay it off.

Tommy had kept in touch with Bobby Campbell and Smooth Simon and each now worked for Tommy full time, issuing loans and collecting the interest and full payments. Neither were thinking men but they were both 'handy' should they need to be, and could follow orders well enough.

Business was booming. Hartlepool was in a full blown recession. The ship yards no longer open. The North works, one of the 2 steel works in Hartlepool already shut, with the South works having most of its plant mothballed.

Bobby and Simon both worked hard for Tommy. Neither had fared well, since Billy's demise and the folding of the gang, both ending up as bouncers and taxi drivers. Tommy made sure they were well rewarded for their efforts and that they could account for every penny they should have collected.

Smooth Simon though, had a death wish.

Just before 5pm on a Thursday evening, a huge slab of a man burst into the domestic appliance rental shop on Park Road. Fortunately, Tommy was there using the back office as his own when the man arrived.

"Where is he? I will fucking kill him. Where the fuck is he?" the man shouted.

The guy, who Tommy later found out was called Paul Begley, ran into the back office. His face red, spittle flying from his mouth as he shouted.

"Whoa" shouted Tommy, "calm down fella and be quick about it."

"Calm down, calm fucking down. Where is that cunt Simon? I will show you calm." Paul picked up a desk lamp and smashed it on the wall.

Despite being at least three inches shorter, Tommy was at least twenty years younger and six stone lighter. He hit the man mountain quickly, once in the face to stun him and three good body shots to slow him down. Paul Begley went down like a bag of shite.

"Now, here! Sit against the wall, drink this water, and tell me what the fuck is going on?" said Tommy, kneeling next to Paul Begley.

"Our Julie, me daughter, took a loan out with you lot. She's missed one payment and you have doubled the debt and that cunt Simon, has also had her suck him off. She's twenty nine, for fucks sake, just trying to make her way in the world as a single mum."

"OK" said Tommy "I don't have the foggiest what you are talking about but let's find out shall we? I promise you now, if what you say is true, then Simon has worked his last day for me."

twenty minutes later, Tommy had established that Julie Begley had taken a loan from Simon and not from Flounders rentals and loans. Simon was charging more than double the interest, than he should be, and pocketing the lot. The loan card was very similar but not the same, an unsuspecting punter would sign the agreement, believing they were going to be a customer of Tommy's.
Tommy sent Paul Begley on his way, with Julie's original loan money plus another £50, on the understanding that Tommy would deal with Simon. They arranged to meet at Julie's house the following evening. He called Gary, briefed him on what had happened and said that he would deal with it as a priority.
The next morning when Simon and Bobby came into the shop, for the lists of the day's collections and leads, Tommy had Simon stay behind.
"Right Simon. I am going to give you one chance, so you fucking listen to me hard. I fucking know you are fiddling me, I want every loan card you have written for yourself, using your books on this table, within ten minutes or I will give you the pasting of your life."
"Tommy, what the fuck are you on about? I would never do that. You know me, why would I cross you and Gary? This is the best earner I have had, since the gang broke up."
Tommy stood up and walked around the table calmly.
"Simon" said Tommy resting his hands on Simon's shoulders, "listen to me. We go way back, which is why I haven't beat you to a fucking pulp, but if you do not give me every fucking card you have, right now, I will break bones. Please trust me. I want to make this as easy as I can for you but do not fucking lie to me. Now go get those fucking cards."

Simon went to say something, appeared to think better of it and went out to his car. Three minutes later he was back and laid five cards on Tommy's desk.
Julie Begley's was amongst them. Tommy quickly added up the payments made and what was outstanding, four of the five cards had already paid twice the value of the loan and still owed more than the original loan as they had defaulted a week's payments. This was loan sharking at its worst and it was done under Tommy's name.
"Right come on then let's do your round."
Simon had twenty calls to make for collection and five new leads to follow up. Outside of the first call of the day Tommy stopped Simon.
 "Right, tell Mrs Bland that you are leaving the business and that I will be taking over the collections, until we find your replacement."
"What the fuck, come on Tommy. I made a mistake is all, I won't do it again, I promise. I just have a lot of debt, you know, and I have worked so hard. I thought if I just get myself straight it would be ok, that's all I was doing Tommy. I didn't want to rip you off."
Tommy knocked on Mrs Bland's door.
 "You fucking tell her and make no mistakes." Two minutes later, the money collected and the message delivered, they drove to the next house. Before lunch, all collections were made and all messaged delivered.
"Right Simon do you have your bank book with you?"
"No why?"
"Because you owe the five punters you mugged over, £68 between them and I aint fucking paying it."
"Tommy, I have nothing. Honest I am brassic. I'm kipping round me mums again. Can't even afford a flat."

"Right then, back to the office and we can write you out a card. I will loan you the £68, then go and clear up the mess you have started."

The tension in the office was palpable, made worse by Tommy using the same terms and conditions that Simon had for the five people he had taken on himself.

"That's £23 a week for six weeks, for a £68 loan."

" I aint going to be able to pay that Tommy. I have no fucking job remember."

"Not my problem. You will come here every Monday before 10:00 and pay up. If you default, I will deal with you personally. Now fuck off."

Tommy had Bobby pick up the five leads he had and then visited the four borrowers that he had not met, explained that Simon had not been working for him, when he set up the loan agreements, and refunded them every penny they had paid, writing off their debt at the same time.

"We advertise in the Hartlepool Mail all the time and our rates are always in the ad. Feel free to come to the office if you need help again, and ask for me. I will do a better than the advertised deal for you" he told each of his wronged customers.

Reputation was everything for Tommy. He saw himself as hard but fair. He knew that word would soon get out that Flounders was a name that could be trusted and that he would right a wrong. Tommy was absolutely fuming with Simon but his business brain knew that this would probably work well for him.

When people found out what had happened and how Tommy had not only resolved the issue but paid back every penny people had paid, he would be recognised as a fair man.

At 5pm as arranged, he arrived at Julie Begley's house to meet with her and her father.

Paul Begley opened the door.

"All sorted then," he asked.

"Yes. Can I come in for a minute? I would like to apologise personally to your daughter."

Julie Begley was a single mum, living in a two up two down terraced street, over on the West View Estate. The house was sparsely furnished but clean, smelling of a mixture of washing and cooking. It was homely and Tommy felt immediately comfortable in the surroundings, reminding him so much of his mum's house, where he occasionally still slept, when he wasn't in his own house on the new Clavering Estate.

"Julie, I wanted to meet you personally to apologise. Simon Rippingale was an employee of mine when he fraudulently sold you the loan. I feel some responsibility for the distress he has put you through. During my investigation today, I have found four other families that he has issued similar loans to. All have had their payments returned and their debt cancelled.

Simon was unable to pay me for the sum of those loans, which was £68 in total. So, I have lent him the money, at the same interest rate he was charging you. Which means he is paying £23 a week. I would like to offer you the following, as way of further compensation and as a thank you for being brave enough to tell your father what was going on. I can either pay you £23 a week, starting today, or £68 now. I know this will not make better the trauma you have been through but I can't unmake what has happened."

"Take the £68 love" chipped in Paul Begley "it's a lot of money."

"£138 is a lot more Dad. Would I be ok to take the £23 a week Mr Flounders?"

"Of course you would love, and that is the decision I would have made."

Tommy could see a pile of Hornby model cars in one corner.

"Are they your son's?" he asked.

"Yes. Our Terry's. He's going to be 11 next week and I'll be able to have a proper party for him now, thanks to you."

"Really? What day are you having the party?" Tommy asked.

"Saturday afternoon, would you like to come Mr Flounders?"

"Unfortunately, I have a prior appointment" (the thought of a room full of screaming kids sending a shudder down his spine) "but I do know Tony Amerigo. I will have one of his ice cream vans pull up at 3pm, for free ice creams all round, if you would like that?"

"Really? That would be lovely. Thank you so much."

Tommy then addressed Paul Begley.

"I hope you can see I was sincere Mr. Begley. The only thing I have not done, is lay hands on Simon. He will need to work hard to pay off the debt and he will not be able to do that if he is in hospital. I understand your anger but would advise you not to look for him. If you were to beat him up and get caught by the Police, you may end up behind bars. You are a family man Mr Begley, not a criminal."

Paul Begley shrugged his shoulders.

"Maybe you are right Tommy. I have murder in my bones right now, so not seeing him, might be best for all."

Julie Begley gave her dad's arm a squeeze.

"Thanks dad. It is for the best and thank you Mr Flounders."

Feeling very happy with himself, Tommy paid Julie her first instalment of £23 and left for home.

20

Months passed for Tommy and business boomed. He recruited someone else to take over Simon's patch and the business rolled in. Of course, he had defaulters but mostly people paid on time and in full. After all, everyone knew Tommy was a good man, but a hard man.
Saturday nights were always a big night out for Tommy. On one Saturday, late in the year, with the wind and rain battering the windows, he decided to stop in.
Gary would be seeing his bird, which he was doing more and more these days. If he bumped into Bobby or anyone else that worked for him and Gary, he would be tapped up for free drinks and would have to listen to how he could run his business better. So, he settled down, got a Chinese take away, chicken curry, chips and rice, and was watching Match of the Day, when there was a knock at the door. Geoff Hornby, who was a constable with the old bill, stood on the door step. Immediately Tommy sensed there was something wrong.
"What is it Geoff?" he asked.
"I'm sorry Tommy, it's your old man. Someone jumped him on the way back from the club. He's in hospital now. He's taken a right pasting."
"Fuck sake! Do you know who?" asked Tommy, lacing his boots on and grabbing a jacket.
"Not at the moment Tommy but we will do everything we can to find out. Do you want a lift over?"
"Nah, you're ok Geoff. I will take the motor and thank you, I owe you one for coming straight over."
It would have been easier for Geoff to drive him but Tommy just didn't like coppers and he needed his car, just in case his dad knew who jumped him.
When he arrived, his mum was already at the hospital and she fell into his arms crying.

"Tommy sweetheart, he's in surgery. He has a broken leg and they are worried about his liver."
"It will be ok mum. Me dads as tough as shoe leather. The pasting he's given his liver over the years, with the booze, a bit of a kicking won't make a lot of difference. Did you get to speak to him mum?"
"Just briefly son, as they were wheeling him to the theatre."
"Did he see who did it?"
"No son. He was jumped from behind. He thinks they had a pick axe handle or something like that. Why would anyone do this to your dad Tommy?"
"I don't know mum but the bizzies will find out for us."
'Unless I find out first' he thought.

21

Fortunately, his dad made a full recovery. He spent 3 days in hospital, another 5 recuperating at home and then when he was strong enough, wandered out on his crutches for a pint, as if nothing had happened. Those that knew Tommy senior well, greeted him and asked how he was. Then took the piss for the rest of the time he was out, telling him he probably fell over his own shoe laces. When Tommy senior wandered off home, after a couple of beers, the guys that had been sat around the table with him all agreed he had changed. He had a vulnerable air about him, that they had never seen before. All of a sudden, he seemed to have aged ten years.

Tommy spent the next couple of days visiting every pub in the area that his father took the beating in, and all the pubs in the town centre. He spoke to every manager promising them, and any member of staff, that heard anything about what had happened, a good reward if they called him and not the coppers. He did keep in touch with the Police, although their enquires didn't go anywhere.

Tommy was still a face. He still looked after coppers. Always donated to their charity nights and had helped out more than one when they were short, issuing interest free loans. He had no doubt that should the right copper hear a whisper, they would tip him off.

22

Over two months after his father had been turned over, Tommy took an unexpected visit from Omar.
"Tommy" he boomed, his face beaming. "It is so good to see you." He gave Tommy a bear hug before kissing him on each cheek.
Tommy could not help but be enthused by seeing Omar. He always greeted him like a long-lost son, and although nearly all of Tommy's activities these days were legitimate and well-paying, he still missed the cut and thrust of illicit activity. The adrenalin rush that a man got, when he out witted the plod.
Omar, whilst never going into too much detail, always held court with Tommy, regaling him with the Turks gangs most recent escapades. Tommy always left their meetings feeling elated and not a little jealous of Omar's lifestyle. Today, instead of going to one of Omar's barber shops for a dark coffee, Omar ushered Tommy into his car.
"You still have the yard, Tommy?"
"Yes of course."
Omar instructed his chauffer in Turkish and they set off for the yard.
"It might be wise when we get there, to give your boys the afternoon off Tommy."
Once they were at the yard and Tommy's 2 guys had left for the day, a small van pulled onto the premises. Two of Omar's guys got out and closed the gates behind them, as Omar led Tommy to the back of the van. He opened the doors and huddled up in a corner, gagged and bound, lay Smooth Simon. One eye had a slight cut over it but other than that, he looked in good health.
"This sikitr (Omar often used his mother tongue when swearing) was sat in one of our dens, using our product

and telling his cronies how he beat your father up Tommy. This is your man. We picked him up 3 hours ago. It was clean, nobody saw us. Do what you wish with him, there will be no comebacks."

Simon who had been listening shook his head violently trying to talk.

"Is your man sure Omar?"

"I would not be here Tommy if I were not sure. He is your man."

Tommy reached into the van and dragged Simon out by his feet. Looking down at him, he felt a rage the likes of which he had never felt before. It took all his self-control to not kick the shit out of Simon, right there and then. Tommy turned to Omar, "I will be forever in your debt, thank you my friend."

Omar pushed a slip of paper into Tommy's hand. "The names of the guys he was talking to, although I am satisfied they were not involved. This fool has loose lips. He was bragging about what he had done. He acted alone my friend."

23

Fifteen minutes later, Omar and his men had left. Tommy and Simon were in the windowless office of the portacabin, where Tommy had already taken one life. Tommy had made a cup of tea and sat sipping it, as he watched Simon, watching him.
Tommy made and drank the tea to give himself time to calm down. The simple function of making the tea allowed him to focus before he spoke to Simon. To gather his thoughts and to restrain himself from simply killing Simon where he sat.
"Simon" said Tommy, "I will have my say. I want you to understand what I am thinking, what I am feeling before I let you talk. You need to focus now, as if your life depends on it." Tommy left the words hanging in the air.
"I gave you a job Simon. I gave you purpose, a reason to get up in the morning. A better wage than most earn in this town. I gave you this, as a friend. I asked for nothing back, other than you do your job and remain loyal.
You threw all of this back in my face." Simon shook his head and tried to speak through the gag.
"I said fucking listen Simon. You can't listen, if you try to speak. You Simon, you took advantage of my good will. You took money from me, you shafted me, you hurt my business reputation. You violated a young woman in my name. You charged excessive interest rates to the most vulnerable of people. You fucking betrayed me Simon. Had you come to me, explained the situation you were in, I would have loaned you the money but you tried to be smart. You tried to bite the hand that fed you. That was stupid beyond words."
Simon could see Tommy was bristling, his body looked pumped, like he had just had a workout. Tommy looked

lethal, and yet he seemed to be as calm as Simon had ever seen him.

"Remember back in the day Simon, when Billy told you all I was part of the top table, his number 2. You questioned that, I saw it in your eyes then Simon, I saw the hate. Still, I trusted you, gave you a job and you turned me over. Like I was a nobody, like I was not someone to be fucking feared. I let you off lightly. Now I realise, too lightly. I should have broken your hands, broken your fucking fingers but I didn't, I was weak. And how did you repay me Simon? You beat my fucking Father up. Attacked him from behind, not even a fucking fair fight. You were too much of a coward to try to hurt me, you picked on an old arthritic man."

Simon shook his head, eyes full of tears.

"Don't fucking deny it Simon. If you try to tell me one fucking lie, you will not leave here alive. Now of course, I have to decide what to do, and you will help with that. I am going to take the gag off and you will speak. You will have your moment to help me understand, what the fuck you were thinking, but be warned! One fucking lie and I will fucking kill you where you sit, do you understand?"

Simon, head down nodded. A minute later he was drinking water from a cup Tommy held for him, his hands still bound behind his back.

"Now talk. Tell me what the fuck you thought you were doing, you cunt!"

Simon shook his head, tears flowing freely dropping from the long eyelashes that had helped seduce so many women.

"Tommy I am sorry. When you sacked me, I lost everything. I even had to sell my clothes to make the last payment. I tried to get door work but was turned away. The Turks would not use me, I couldn't get a job, and me habit was costing me a bomb. I did a bit of robbing and fencing to get by, I even worked the sea coal wagons for a bit but me life was shit. I was off me face, when I saw your dad. He was laughing and joking having a good time. It was the drugs Tommy, they just sent me mad. I got so angry and when he left, I followed him. I didn't mean to hurt him, Tommy, honest I didn't. I just wanted to give him a bit of a slappin', is all."

A sob burst from his lips, a snot bubble doing the same from his nose. Tommy felt no pity. Simon was the second person he knew personally, that had fucked their life through drugs, but even worse, this one had hurt his family.

"Look at the fucking state of you. You could have had it all Simon. Good job, nice clothes, a place to live, everything you fucking wanted. I was paying you above rates and would have increased it, as the business grew but instead you tried to fuck me over. Then when I rumbled you, you took a side swipe at me dad. Why didn't you come looking for me? You know where I live. You know where I work. You want to hurt someone you could have come for me. Why didn't you?"

Simon just sat on the floor, head down, silent tears falling from his eyes.

"Nothing to say? Alright then, here's what's going to occur. If you walk out of that gate, back out onto the street we are done. You never darken my door. If you see my family, any of them, you cross the road. You stay away for me and mine, and I stay away from you."

Simon looked up at Tommy

"But, you little fucking toe rag, to do that you have to get past me first. This is it in a nutshell Simon, make no mistake. You will be fighting for your life."

"What do you mean Tommy?"

"What I mean is, I am going to cut that rope from your wrists and ankles. then we fight. If you manage to get past me, to the gate you are free. If you don't, you die."
"Fuck off Tommy. You know I can't fight you."
"Time to learn then and you have a real good reason to do it."
Tommy took an old Stanley knife from a drawer and dragged Simon out of the portacabin, into the yard. It was almost dusk. The trading estate around them, was quiet.
After unlocking the yard gate, Tommy cut the rope that had held Simon's wrists and feet and put the knife on an old oil drum.
"Just to make it fair" he said to Simon, who was trying to rub some life blood into his wrists and hands, "I will give you the first shot" Tommy stood between Simon and the gate. "Whenever you are ready," he said, quiet menace in his voice.
Simon's eyes were dancing between Tommy and the gate, just 20 yards to freedom.
"Can't we do this another way?" he asked
"No Simon, we can't."
Before Tommy had even got the words out of his mouth, Simon threw an overhand right. He tried to dodge around Tommy and head for the gate. Tommy was ready though. He had spent so many years sparring, boxing and street fighting, he almost knew what Simon was going to do before he did. Tommy stepped aside from the telegraphed punch and threw a low right of his own, catching Simon hard in the gut. Before he could take his first step to freedom, Simon went down like a sack of spuds.
"Up you get fella" said Tommy, as he lifted a winded wheezing Simon to his feet.

"Christ mate" he said, "I thought you would be a bit better than that. This isn't going to be much of a fight is it. I am going to be able to beat the crap out of you, without trying. Maybe we should try to make it a bit more even, it's so unfair. Perhaps I should tie one hand to my side? Oh, but wait a fucking minute, my dad had his back to you. Did he not? How fair was that?"

Tommy then went to work. Two punches and Simon was on the floor, a nasty cut open over one eye. Tommy sat astride of him and worked his face mercilessly.

Boxers wear boxing gloves for 2 reasons. The primary reason boxing gloves are used in the sport, is to protect the boxer's hand from injuries. The bones of the hand are small and delicate, allowing people to use their fingers and hands for precise movements, such as catching, drawing, or writing. In contrast, the skull's only purpose is to protect and contain one of the most important and fragile organs in the human body, the brain.

Because of this, the skull is the hardest bone in the body. Striking another person's head with delicate hands results in injured hands and the bones within them.

The impact of the force in a moving object is known as momentum—boxing is all about momentum. Without boxing gloves, the effect of the momentum can be more effective than with gloves. Without gloves, the momentum a punch can carry may result in heavy damage and a severe injury to your opponent. Tommy knew all of this, he knew his hands were taking damage. He could feel bones breaking but he kept hammering down relentlessly, on Simon's now blood covered face. Simon's hands lay motionless by his side. Tommy punched until he was exhausted and then stopped. Sat across his man. looking down on a face that no one would now recognise, he winced in pain at the self-

inflicted damage he had done to himself. He believed he had killed Simon but to his surprise, and astonishment, Simon's chest was still rising and falling.
Twenty minutes later, Simon was in the boot of an old Austin 11, that sat inside the compactor. The boot lid was open and Tommy stood outside. with a bucket of water. He soaked Simon, who slowly regained consciousness. Awake but not really alert, one eye rolled back in his head, the other almost shut with swelling.
"Simon, can you hear me buddy? Fuck, I can't believe you are still alive. Can you hear me pal? You don't have to talk, just grunt, or wave a hand or something."
Simon did just that. His right hand strangely undamaged, when compared to Tommy's swollen knuckles, moved a little, just to signal he was listening.
"And you understand me ok?"
Again, a twitch of a hand.
 "You got a fucking hard head, I will give you that pal. Me hands are wrecked, properly wrecked. You know, when I killed Billy, I did it when he was unconscious."
Simon mewled, an almost feline sound, half scared half confused.
"Yes buddy. It was me that killed him. I had to. He was ripping off the Turks. Anyway, where was I? Ah yeah. When I killed him, he was unconscious. Spaced out of his fucking head, on those fucking drugs that he used so much. I was glad at the time. I didn't want him to know what was going on.
But you, you fucker, I want you to know for sure what is going on. So, this" and Tommy lifted a 2lb hammer, "this will be the way, I finally break that fucking thick skull of yours. Now I don't know if you can see this, your eyes look pretty fucked up, but here feel." Tommy lay the ball pein of the hammer in Simon's hand, that had moved seconds before. Simon's hand moved slightly, to cup the

hammer end rather than actually grip it, he whimpered again.

"This is a lesson, not for you but for me. A lesson I have to learn. It was foolish of me to fight you, so never again. The evidence of our fight is on my hands and I will carry those wounds for the rest of my life. If the coppers were to come looking for you, which they won't, it would be hard to explain what happened to my hands. So, I am grateful for the lesson. This is it, Simon. This is what is going to happen. I am going to bray your fucking skull in, with this hammer, close the boot on your pitiful wreck of a body and compact this fucking car to a 4 foot square. Next Wednesday, it will be taken away and smelted down.

No funeral pal, no grieving parents or friends. No kind words said by people who hardly knew you, who never liked you, no wake. You will simply be gone. The space that you once polluted, by being alive, will be filled with fresh air. You crossed a line pal, twice, and now you pay."

A blood red tear wandered down the swollen cheek, below the closed eye, on Simon's face. That was the last physical action Simon ever took.

Tommy gripped the hammer as hard as he could, grimacing with pain shooting from his broken hand and he finished Simon. Hitting him until his skull was so misshapen, it was almost hard to recognise it for what it was. Tommy closed the lid of the boot on Simon, and on the freshly wiped down hammer, compacted the car, and closed a chapter of his life.

'If ever I have to do something like this again,' he thought to himself, 'it has to be cleaner, less personal.'

After crushing the car, quickly checking it to make sure no evidence of Simon was apparent, he stacked it with the rest in the yard.

He had killed 2 men on these premises and, as far as he was aware, disposed of a 3rd. 'Pretty useful things, scrap yards!'

Tommy wished he could tell his dad that his attacker had been dealt with, but if he did his dad would want details. So, as was his way, he was cautious and said nothing.

24

The following Monday, Tommy visited the Square Circle Pub, behind the College of Further Education in town. As he expected, Brian Long was sat in a corner of the bar, Racing Times open in front of him with rolled cigarette dangling from his lips. Tommy ordered a soft drink for himself and a pint of Strongarm with a large whiskey chaser for Brian and wandered over to the table. Setting the drinks to the side of the paper and sitting opposite Brian.

"Now then Tommy" said Brian, looking down at the drinks, then across to Tommy. "It's been about eight years since I clapped eyes on you, and here you are giving me free drinks, like you want to get into my fucking pants. What do you want?"

Tommy laughed out loud. "Nowts changed then Brian. Still such a warm human being, full of the joys of simply being alive."

"Aye, I am so fucking happy, I walk around with a permanent semi. It's good to see you boy, but what do you want?"

Tommy lifted his hands and put them on the table. Both hands had blue knuckles, they were swollen and cut.

"Fuck me Tommy, been punching walls?"

"You might say that, Brian. Truth is, it's me own fault. I have had them wrapped and on ice most of the weekend but I need a good break man to take care of these. You have been a cut man for over forty years. You know every surgeon in the area. Who would you recommend?"

Brian sucked his teeth, downed the shot of whiskey and said "Dr Shafaq Hussain, out of Newcastle. He's a fucking Paki but he has rebuilt hands, better than anyone I have seen. But you know they are fucked don't ya? No doctor can fix the unfixable, and he aint fucking cheap either."

"I aint worried about the price Brian. Money is no object and yeah, every time I punched another hole in that wall, I knew I was fucking myself up."

Tommy laid £25 on the table. "Here have a bet on me and thank you."

Brian looked down at the crisp notes, sniffed, looked back up at Tommy and said "I thought Money was no fucking object!"

For the second time that day Tommy laughed, adding another £20 to the pile, he said "Good to see you too buddy," and walked out of the pub.

Brian watched him leave. He pocketed the money and thought to himself, 'I pity the fucker who was on the end of that.'

25

Three days later, Tommy sat in a plush office in the centre of Newcastle. Dr Hussain was much younger than Tommy had imagined, perhaps in his mid to late 30's. He spoke with a Midlands accent. His desk had a sliver photo frame of a wife and 2 small children. On the wall, along with medical certificates, were a number of photographs of Dr Hussain cradling some sort of rifle in his hands.

"Mr Flounders, do you bare knuckle box? These are some of the worst injuries I have seen, outside of industrial injuries."

Tommy was wary of saying too much "No Doctor. I was attacked outside of a night club by a couple of guys. They were drunk but persistent, I had to defend myself quite vigorously."

Dr Hussain gave Tommy an appraising look, "I fear for the men who took you on Mr Flounders but that is their concern not mine.

Now to business. We will need to x-ray your hands and then determine what treatment is necessary. My receptionist will take you down to the x-ray suite. If you would like to come back tomorrow, at the same time, we will discuss how to move forwards."

"Could I just ask before I go Doctor. That rifle you are holding. Is that a real one?"

"Yes, I am a member of a firearms club at Catterick Army Garrison. Under the controlled conditions they provide, we can use pistols and rifles, with live ammunition."

"That sounds very interesting. How does a person go about joining?"

"You would need to apply to the courts for a licence first. It is a simple process, providing you do not have a criminal record. If you get your licence, I would happily take you to the club, as a guest."

"Thank you, Doctor. See you tomorrow."

The prognosis could have been a lot worse for Tommy. The results of the x-rays showed 2 fractures on the right hand and 1 on the left. None of which required surgery although his fingers would be strapped together, for a few weeks.

A few days later, Tommy had a pint with one of the Police officers he had become friendly with. It turned out that applying for a licence was simple enough and as Tommy was fortunate enough to have never been arrested in his early years, there would be no reason not to grant a licence. The Licensing officer, a Sargent Phil Kenny, was known vaguely to Tommy. They had met at a couple of charity events, that Tommy's business had help sponsor. He even helped Tommy correct a couple of issues on his application and within 4 weeks, Tommy had a licence to carry and store a shotgun and cartridges. He could also use pistols and rifles, at approved facilities, although he could not take them from site or own them.

On a cold day, in January 1980, Shaf as Tommy now knew Dr Hussain, signed himself and Tommy onto the gun range at Catterick Garrison.

It had turned out that Shaf was looking to invest in property. Tommy and Gary Tanners had spent some time with him, talking through the pros and cons, before identifying what they thought would be prime off plan investment opportunities in the domestic market. Gary Tanners would be able to arrange the purchase process for him, along with managing the rentals. During this time, Tommy and Shaf had become friends and Shaf was more than happy to sign Tommy onto the range.

Tommy provided his gun licence and 2 other forms of ID to the administration team at the range and was then allowed to go with Shaf, into the range itself.
Firstly, Shaf signed out two Browning 9mm handguns. Standard sidearm issue for the British forces, it held a magazine of thirteen rounds. Paper targets were placed 10m from a shooting booth and Shaf began to coach Tommy on the use of the weapon. Immediately after Tommy's first shot, he was hooked. The following week, his application for membership to the gun club was in. Three weeks later it was approved. Tommy was a member of the range.
By now, he was competent with a handgun and had passed an assessment which with his membership, allowed him to draw handguns and use them unaccompanied.
Tommy though, was desperate to try a rifle and booked three 2 hour lessons with one of the Army instructors, that worked at the range part time.
Lieutenant John 'Jacko' Jackson, was five years older than Tommy and they hit it off immediately. Jacko was shorter than Tommy at about 5'11" tall. He had a ruddy face with a square jaw and a number one beard and haircut. His hair was redder than his complexion. He was stocky with broad shoulders and muscular forearms, that danced as he moved his hands. His waist probably carried a little fat but he was not a man that would go down to a gut punch. More the kind of man that would become annoyed by one.
He was dressed in army fatigues, sleeves rolled up above the elbow. He was clearly a confident man, but there was no arrogance to him. He chatted to Tommy like they had known each other for years and was able to communicate the complexity of using a rifle easily and confidently. The first lesson was mainly classroom and

was about the use and maintenance of the standard army issue rifle the L1A1 SLR (self loading rifle). The 7.6mm cartridge was effective up to 800 yards or 'half a fucking mile,' as Jacko put it.

Tommy, after already being around handguns, proved a good student and because of that, they were able to go out onto the range at the end of the first lesson. The targets were set at 200 yards and Tommy got to fire his first shot. He was absolutely hooked. The lesson ran twenty minutes and thirty rounds over. Jacko was a gem. "We're the fucking army mate. We lose tanks, never mind the odd fucking bullet," he replied, when Tommy asked if he needed to fork out for the extra cartridges. Tommy took Jacko for a beer afterwards and a friendship began, that has lasted both men all of their lives.

26

Over the next two years, Tommy became more than proficient with both handguns and rifles. He excelled at the rifle, regularly shooting targets accurately from over 600 yards. Jacko also got Tommy onto a training site one Sunday morning. It was a group of derelict buildings, that had friend and enemy dummies popping up all over the place. Tommy had loved it and excelled, not once shooting a friendly dummy. He never felt more alive than when he had a pistol in his hand.
In April 1982, Jacko got notice he was destined to go to join the Falklands task force, that was due to set sail from Portsmouth. He and Tommy had a last drink, away from barracks, in a pub called The Hildyard Arms in Catterick.
"This is what I joined up for. Protecting Queen and Country and all that but I kinda wish I weren't going. I've gotten lazy Tommy. Still, I need the extra money I will earn for sure, I am fucking brassic mate."
"How much do you need?" was the instant response from Tommy.
"Nothing from you, although you ever need to arm yourself, let me know," he said, half jokingly."
"If you're serious, I will have a couple of pistols and a rifle off you, with 200 rounds for each."
"You serious?"
"Damn serious. I will store them at the scrap yard I own. You never know when a gun might come in handy and if I get caught with them, I will blame the last owner of the yard."
"Are you sure Tommy? It's going to be a piece of piss for me to get them out. There has never been a better time, but I don't want to be taking them back with me because you get cold feet."

89

"Name the price, the place, the day and time and I will be there cash in hand buddy."

Two days later, Tommy had collected 2 browning 9mm's and 1 L1A1 SLR, complete with day and night scopes and 600 rounds of ammunition split 400 / 200, in favour of the pistols. It has cost him £500. A fucking bargain, as far as he was concerned.

The workshop in Tommy's scrap yard is huge and there are a number of old inspection pits along with a heavy duty car lift. Tommy chose one of the inspection pits, as far from the workbenches as possible. He lifted a few floor boards, made from old railway sleepers that covered the pits. He wrapped the guns in oil cloth and stored them in the pit, replacing the sleepers.

The next day he purchased and parked an old Range Rover over the pit.

"It's a restoration project' he told his yard men, 'keep your fucking hands off it."

Every Sunday without fail, Tommy would lift the boards from the pit. Strip, oil and reassemble the guns before heading off to Catterick for some target practice, using legitimate guns on the range.

Jacko returned to Catterick in August of eighty two. He and Tommy set the town alight in Hartlepool, downing more beer that Tommy could ever remember. Jacko didn't talk much, about what went on over there, other than to complain that the army was still run by public schoolboys, who loved to play soldier and that the equipment they were provided with was 'shite.'

Later that year, Jacko left the Army after twenty years' service. The army was the only life he had known. He had signed up, just after he left school. Jacko knew no other life, or work, but Tommy recognised something in him. So, he offered him a job, as executive director, of the betting shops.

"It's a piece of piss" explained Tommy, when Jacko asked if he was sure of the job offer. "All of the shops run like clockwork, now I have sorted out the staffing. It's simply a matter of double checking the books and doing some quick audits. I will be able to teach you in a day. You army boys love your routine. This is simply routine but in jeans not cammo's."

Gary Tanners was more than happy to have Jacko on board. Both he and Tommy had been working hard on the business, ploughing most of the profits back into it, to grow it as quickly as they could. A spare pair of hands would allow them to focus more on areas of the business that needed their attention, and hopefully reduce the hours he was working. He was now married, with 2 small children and a lovely house on the headland, facing out to sea. With someone who Tommy trusted looking out for the bookies, that was one less thing to worry about.

27

In March of 1983, Omar took tea with Tommy. He was, as ever, graceful and eloquent. Towards the back end of their two hours together, Omar asked Tommy a question that he had been dreading but felt sure would come one day.
"Tell me Tommy, was it you that planned the raid on the nightclub back in sixty six?" Tommy knew there was nothing to be gained by lying and he respected Omar too much to even consider it.
"Yes Omar, it was. I was not quite sixteen and Billy wanted to go in, all guns blazing, when you were open. It would have been a blood bath. I changed his mind. So yes, it was my plan."
Omar looked at Tommy for a few seconds.
"I never thought it was Billy who hit us. He came to us on the Monday, trying to buy more dope, even though you had robbed us of so much. He just wasn't that smart and it was too clever for him. He was common, a thug, no finesse but now I understand why it went so well, the boy was teaching the man. You must understand Tommy, I bear you no ill will. Business is business and mutually, for many years now, we have made money together. I trust and like you but I know what you did because one of my men brought a user to me. He had run up a considerable debt and asked to pay it off by informing who carried out the raid. You are pretty much the only person, of significance, left from Billy's gang. There are men in my organisation who want to make an example of you.
My position is weak now Tommy. I have 4 lieutenants Alp, Emre, Selim and Mehmet. It is tradition that a President like me steps down when he hits sixty. I am sixty four Tommy. Selim and Mehmet have designs on

my role. They work well together but are ruthless and they want to come after you. Alp and Emre respect my wishes, I have said you were merely a boy at the time and should not be held responsible, as you did not run the gang, and that over the years you have more than paid us back.

I have cancer my friend. If I am lucky, I will see the Autumn but it is doubtful I will live that long. Selim and Mehmet will either kill me or wait until I die but either way they will come after you, once I am dead. In this folder is up to date information on them both. Many men owe me favours Tommy, and many are still loyal, they will remain so after my death. It is only these two you need to worry about. You will see that, along with their home addresses, are the places they meet regularly, bars, restaurants but particularly a small unit on an industrial estate. They are shipping stolen luxury cars from there. This should have been declared to me but they disrespect me, they keep all of the profits to themselves. I know they plot against me. Once I am gone. the way we do things will change. We will lose our finesse, we will become common thugs.

I believe they are also using the unit to plan how they will run things, when I am gone. They are fools Tommy, too ambitious. Each will be planning the others demise, even as they slap each other's back and share a drink. You cannot move against these men while I live, but if you act swiftly when I die it will be seen as in fighting or, if I am murdered, retribution for my killers. Be careful Tommy, leave no trail back to you and you may yet live a long life.

This is the last time we take tea. I am frail and need to make plans for my family when I am gone.

You are a thinker, Tommy." Omar grinned "Tommy the thinker. I believe this is not the first time I have called you this. Plan well Tommy. Now I must go."
They both stood, embraced for the last time, Tommy's eyes spilling over with tears.
"Don't cry Tommy. Plan," said Omar, as they walked to his car.
"This is the one person you can trust, his name is Burak" said Omar, pointing to his driver who stood outside of the car, smoking an acrid smelling Turkish cigarette.
"When the time comes, he will let you know I have passed. Be ready and act swiftly. Avenge me, and protect yourself. Goodbye my friend."
With that, Omar stepped into his car and out of Tommy's life.
A couple of hours later, Tommy and Jacko sat in the portacabin at the scrapyard, going over the file Omar had left.
It was comprehensive, colour and black and white pictures of both men. Their home addresses plus layouts of their houses. The bars they frequented, the times they normally visited them and where they chose to sit. Each owned more than one car, these were detailed, including registration numbers.
Of most interest to Tommy and Jacko, was the small unit they had on an industrial estate in Southbank, a small rundown area of Middlesbrough.
The life of a mobster, is to leave the house late and be late home. Omar's lieutenants would mainly meet after 5pm, for an update from their soldiers. They would collect money and hand out drugs, for the next day's deliveries. They would visit bars they owned, brothels and drug dens. Ensuring that all was in order before retiring to the club until the early morning, drinking and fucking.

Selim and Mehmet followed this pattern except, every day they met at the unit at around noon. Normally Selim arriving first, Mehmet any time within 30 minutes but as far as the information Tommy had, they never arrived together.

"That is where I hit them" said Tommy, "it has to be there."

"You hit them? We hit them. You are a brother to me. I have killed, it comes easy to me. You may freeze when the time comes."

"There's no worries about me freezing Jacko, trust me on that. Are you sure you want to come along?"

"Of course, these fuckers know you, not me. It should be me that follows the first fucker in. Once I have dealt with him, then you join me."

"Right, let's go and have a look at this place. See the lie of the land."

Fifty minutes later, they were parked on the opposite side of the road and further up from the unit. There was little chance of the Turks being there, as it was early evening, but they were in boiler suits and a transit van just in case.

"This is ok" said Jacko, "plenty of places to park. Two ways onto a main road. Simple enough job if nothing goes wrong."

"Can you get silenced pistols?" Tommy asked to Jacko's great amusement.

"Fuck sake you dumb fucker," he roared, "the British army doesn't have silencers. You have been watching too many gangster movies, you prat. More seriously," Jacko said "what we have to do, is contain the first fucker, then tap them both together. There's quite a lot of engineering around here. A couple of gunshots may not get picked up on. Two shots to the head and off we drive."

"How do we get in?" asked Tommy.
"Open the fucking door, walk in, shouting electricity board. When he shows his stinking Turk face, stick a fucking pistol in it. Hopefully this won't be a problem, according to the info we have. First in leaves the door unlocked for the next one, who locks it behind him."
The layout of the unit was simple and standard. As you entered through the main door, to the left was a door to the workshop area, which had a roller shutter door to the front and an emergency exit in the rear. A small reception area was to the right of the front door, followed by an office area, which contained a single partitioned office. On the floor plan, further down on the right from the front door, were gent's and ladies' toilets. The main office had windows to the front and side, that had blinds in place. There was no visibility into the office, at all.
Jacko spoke. "We get in, subdue the first fucker and get him in the bogs. Whilst we wait for the next one to arrive, we lift the false ceiling in the bogs up. That way, when we cap the fuckers, the sound will go up rather than radiate out."
"What about the second one?"
"We wait in the office and as soon as he opens the door, twat him and get him in the bogs too. As soon as we have them both in there, we shoot them. It would be smarter to use knives, you know, a fucking lot quieter and quiet is clean," said Jacko.
"Yeah, I thought of that but the Turks like to use guns, more macho. You know what those Turk fuckers are like, always banging their fucking chests, like they are Tarzan or summat. We have to make sure it looks like revenge for Omar from within their organisation."
The next evening, Jacko drove out in a transit van and had a quick walk around the outside of the property. It was pretty much as expected, no surprises.

28

The following Monday, as Tommy left for work, Burak was sat outside of his house. Tommy should not have been surprised that Burak knew where to find him but he was still unnerved about how vulnerable it made him feel.
"Tommy it is done, in front of his wife. Two men, ten bullets." A tear rolled down his cheek. "Kill them bastards Tommy."
"I will and I am sorry for your loss." This was the first time in twelve years he had heard Burak speak and the last time he would ever see him.
Tommy and Jacko met up later that morning. They agreed, that there would be no point going to the unit today. The Turks would get together to discuss how to move forwards, who would become responsible for what, now that Omar was dead and in time, who would become the next President.
Tomorrow they would park outside of the unit at 10:00, in case Selim and Mehmet decided to meet early. The following day, to Tommy's surprise, Jacko had an Electricity Board boiler suit on and a small toolbox sat between them on the middle seat of the transit.
"Where the hell did you get the boiler suit?"
"Lad I knew ages ago give it me. I knew this bird once, who liked me to dress up."
"Stop, enough said. Fuck sake, your sex life is like a fucking sewer, it's disgusting. Is there nothing you haven't or won't do?"
"Not that I'm aware of" said Jacko, grinning.
"Any way, if I follow this geezer in unannounced, there is always a chance he will get the jump on me and then we are in shit street. If I walk in shouting, hello electricity board carrying a toolbox and wearing this boiler suit, he

will be less alarmed. People see what they want to see. Also, he won't want a member of the public to see a gun or knife in his hand. It'll be a lot easier to give him a bang on the head, if he aint expecting one."

Time moved incredibly slowly for both Tommy and Jacko, they were full of nervous energy.

"This is the hard time," said Jacko around 11am, "you know something is going to go off but you just have to sit and wait for the order."

Around 11:45, Selim arrived at the unit, driving his Mercedes. He looked relaxed and happy.

Jacko gave it five minutes before he jumped out of the van, toolbox in hand, cosh concealed in his back pocket.

"Give it a minute and follow me in." He walked across the road and pushed the door. As expected, it was unlocked.

Tommy waited for, what seemed like, an agonisingly long minute and then followed his best friend in, simmering with anger, thinking about his dead friend Omar.

"Fuck sake. Where have you been?" grunted Jacko dragging the limp body of Selim along the corridor to the gents. A minute later, Selim had tie wraps around his hands and feet, his mouth was stuffed with a rag and gaffer taped in place, a dark bag over his head.

"Now for the other fucker," said Jacko.

"Give me the cosh" said Tommy "I will do this one. Where did you find this fucker?" He said kicking Selim's limp leg

"In the office past reception."

"Any weapon?"

"Nah, clean."

"OK I will go and wait. You keep an eye on him."

Tommy quickly looked in the workshop space which had three, 7 series BMWs in it, along with an Aston Martin and a Ferrari.

'Nice little earner outside of the family business,' thought Tommy, as he went to the office. He wondered when the Turks had so much going for them, so much money and a fantastic lifestyle, why these two backward, hairy knuckled fuckers, would risk ruining it all. 'Silly twats' he thought. He quickly rifled through the two desks and filing cabinet but there was nothing of any interest.

Ten minutes later, Tommy heard a car pull up and shortly after, the small squat figure of Mehmet strolled into the office. Tommy stood to the side of the door and hit him as hard as he could with the cosh across the top of the head, and he folded like a hand of cards. Just for luck, he hit him one more time. He then went and locked the front door, turning the lights off. 'Belts and braces,' he thought.

Tommy shouted for Jacko and they dragged Mehmet to the toilets, where they strapped and gagged him, and took his wallet. Jacko had relieved Selim of his wallet too. Neither guy had any id on them, all jewellery also removed. Both were now secured, gagged and had black bags over their heads.

Using a mop handle, Jacko went about pushing up and out, all the false roof tiles.

"That will really make a difference?" asked Tommy.

"Yeah, although it won't sound like it in here."

"Right, how do you want to do this?"

"I want the fuckers awake" came the reply, with loathing in his voice. Tommy could not help but think of Omar. He had practically loved the man and these two had gunned him down, in his own home.

"Tommy, whenever we had conflict, our two main priorities were to achieve the task and minimise the risk.

If you wake these up, you maximise risk. Just pull the triggers and walk away. We also have to deal with the cars."
"What do you mean the cars?"
"If we tap these two now, a bullet in the brain each, lock the door and walk away. How many days before the 2 cars outside get reported? How many days before the doors to this place are opened and these 2 mugs are found? If we drop these cars on Normanby Road, leave the keys in the ignition, they will be lifted in a couple of hours. How long then, before the police or the landlord walks in here? Only Omar knew of this place. Their oppo's won't have a clue where to look. Every day these fuckers lay here rotting, is better for us. We have gloves on. If anyone sees us coming in or out, every day that passes, they will remember less and less about us. Don't forget what we are doing here. It is execution. It's life Tommy, no parole."
"So, what do we do then?"
"Double check the binding on these fuckers. Use up every tie wrap and every piece of gaffer tape we have. Tape them together head to feet, use the tie wraps to secure them to each other and then we move the cars. I drive one out, you follow in the van. When I park it up, you take the next left and I walk to you. Two cars, twenty minutes max. I leave the keys in the ignitions, doors unlocked. It will be minutes before some local hoodlum thinks Christmas has come early and has them away. Then we come back and finish the job."
"Makes sense I suppose."
"Tommy, this was my life, remember. Of course it makes fucking sense. Now let's get it done."
Thirty five minutes later, Tommy and Jacko walked back into the unit, locking the door behind them. They made their way to the toilets, guns in their hands.

Selim and Mehmet were exactly where they'd left them. Selim though, was visibly struggling against their bonds.
"I have to do this Jacko. They have to fucking know."
"OK buddy, if you must."
Jacko began to fill one of the sinks with water and when it was full enough, he took the hood that had been put over Mehmet's head, soaked it with cold water and wrung it out in Mehmet's face. It took three visits, before Mehmet began to stir.
"Jesus Tommy. How fucking hard did you hit him?"
"Not hard enough" was the terse reply.
Eventually, Mehmet was conscious enough for Jacko to remove the bindings that held him and Selim together, although they were still secured individually. Jacko swung Mehmet around, to sit next to Selim both now propped against an outside wall.
Their eyes were locked on Tommy, who rested casually against a wash basin.
"Now boys" he said, "I know you recognise me, and I know, you know it was me that organised the raid on the Top House back in the day. I also fucking know you want to kill me for that and I get that. I don't take it personally. What I do take personally though, is that you two waste of space Turkish cunts, killed my friend Omar. How fucking dare you kill a man, who's shadow you could never walk in. So boys, your time is up. Eventually you will be found here, rotting, like the pair of dead rats you are."
Tommy picked up a pair of revolvers, from the sink to the right of him.
"Whoa there. Hang on a minute Tommy. Here, put these on." Jacko opened the tool box he had walked into the unit with and gave Tommy a pair of ear plugs, a set of safety glasses and finally a pair of ear defenders, to sit over the ear plugs in Tommy's ears.

"Put my overalls on too. This aint going to be pretty. I'll wait in the van. Lock the door on the way out" and with that, he left.

Tommy gave Jacko a minute. He knew that he would be covered with blood, and probably brain, but fuck it Omar deserved this. He was his friend, a mentor even, and fuck he would do right by him.

A pistol in his left hand and one in his right, he leaned over the pair of men below him.

"I fucking wish I could do this with my bare hands" he said, as he touched gun barrels to foreheads, before simply pulling the triggers in unison and snuffing out the lives of the traitorous bastards, that had killed his friend. Tommy was deafened by the sound of the 2 pistols and covered in pieces of dead men. He stood took off the safety glasses, his ear defenders and overalls. He turned the overalls inside out and wiped his face and head, as best he could. Picking everything up, he left the toilets. Turning the heating in the unit up to max and on 24 hrs a day, he made his way out of the front door, locking it behind him.

The transit was parked sideways to the entrance, the side door open. Tommy jumped in, closed the door behind him and sat in the dark on the floor, until Jacko stopped half a mile short of the yard. When there was no traffic on the road, he opened the door and Tommy jumped into the passenger seat. He looked presentable enough, as he hopped out of the transit and straight into the office of his scrap yard. There were a few people wandering about but no one paid him any more attention than could be expected.

Jacko locked the door behind them. Each had a strip wash in the sink before liberally cleaning it and the area around it with bleach. All of their clothes, their shoes and the personal effects they had lifted from Selim and

Mehmet, were put into burlap sacks, to be burnt as soon as the yard had closed for the day.

29

"Right Tommy, what I want to do is, to get a couple of the guys I know to shadow you for a week or two. They will follow you around, from the moment you leave your house, until you get back again. Whatever time that is. If the Turks do decide to take a look at you, my guys will see them."
"OK," said Tommy, "it makes sense but what will you tell them?"
"The truth! You shagged a married bird, as you always seem to be doing these days, but this one was married to a face. So, we need to make sure she keeps quiet and that there are no repercussions."
A drive to Catterick and back and Jacko had eight guys working in pairs, shadowing Tommy. Two weeks later, Tommy stood them down, not a sign of anyone following him.
Eight days after that, Emre, one of the two remaining lieutenants of Omar's, came to visit Tommy, at the same time Omar would have. Emre came alone and had little time for pleasantries.
"Tommy, Omar is dead."
"Yes, I know" came the reply, "and I grieve for him."
Emre gave him a hard stare. "I should not be surprised, that you know news about us, before you should."
"I thought of Omar as a friend, as well as a business partner. There are those that were loyal to him, that thought it right that I should know. I am disappointed it was not one of his trusted lieutenants." If Emre felt insulted by Tommy's remark, he did not show it.
"Omar made me pledge that I would take no action over the raid, that you were involved in, back in '66 and I will honour that. There will never be a repeat, you understand this?"

"Our relationship has changed since then, Emre, I do not buy from you. In fact, you buy from me, the shops and goodwill. I am a businessman now Emre. I am happy for you to be the gangster."

"Tommy tell me, do you know the whereabouts of two of my colleagues. They have been missing for a short while now."

"I only know of Omar," came Tommy's reply.

Emre stared again.

'This fucking guy thinks he's Clint Eastwood,' Tommy thought to himself.

"Very well, business as usual" said Emre. "I will not be visiting as Omar did, I have many tasks to attend to and frankly, I don't like you Tommy but you do well for us. We have no problems with any of the shops. You will be paid as normal, goodbye."

"Have a nice day Emre!"

It was a further 3 weeks, before the Northern Echo reported, that 2 badly decomposed bodies had been found, in a small industrial unit at Southbank. The bodies were in such a condition, they would need dental evidence to identify them due to the length of time they had been there and the temperature they had been exposed to, that had served to speed the decomposition process. The police had speculated that it was in gang fighting, due to the stolen cars that were also found at the unit. As hoped, the Police had little to go on. Selim and Mehmet were not identified by the Turks. They were aware that the bodies had been found but due to the circumstances, and the likelihood it was one of their own that pulled the triggers, no contact was made to the Police. Mehmet was a single man and Selim's family were quickly moved out of the country.

A few hands were greased and shortly after, the investigation was wound down and closed, as

unresolved. The Turks were given a council cremation which, thought Tommy, was way too good for them.
For the Turks, it was an uneasy time. Firstly, they had been betrayed by Selim and Mehmet, it was an open secret that they were responsible for Omar's death, but what concerned everyone in the gang was which of them had pulled the trigger. Who amongst them were responsible for the two deaths and more importantly was there to be any more bloodletting? It was many months before the members of the Turkish organisation began to relax, in the company of one another.

30

Later that year, Tommy and Gary Tanners decided to split the business up and go their separate ways. There was no animosity, it just made sense. Tommy was entrepreneurial, moving quickly in and out of businesses and still had his dubious connections to the underworld. Whilst Gary's only expertise was the housing, commercial buildings and rental side of the business. Nearly all of the houses that they owned between them were mortgage free, so they re-mortgaged them. The money went to Tommy and the ownership of the houses to Gary. Tommy kept the bookmakers, the pub, the scrapyard and a number of small commercial retail units on trading estates, along with the shops they had around Hartlepool.
On the day they signed all of the contracts and the money was released to Tommy's personal accounts, they had one last drink together. Tommy sucking on bottles of continental lager, whilst Gary was now a G&T man. They laughed about the old days, agreed that they would keep in touch and have regular piss ups (both knew as they said the words, that this would not happen nearly as regularly as they had planned).
They also knew that if ever they needed to, they could turn to one another. There would always be a huge friendship, just not an active one.
"People change" said Tommy, when they were 5 hours into their session and he could see Gary checking his watch every ten minutes. "Every fucker changes Gary, apart from me. I'm still single, still chasing every bit of skirt in town and still drinking too much. I love you like a brother but you have gone and got all adult on me. Now stop looking at that fucking watch, go get a taxi and get home to your family." They shared one last drunken hug

and went their separate ways. Gary home to an angry wife and Tommy to the next bar.

31

The domestic appliance rental markets had changed over the years with white goods, along with luxury goods, becoming more affordable. Tommy had closed one shop down and turned the other into a computer supply / repair shop. He was the first supplier of computer equipment in the town and although his shop was barely paying its way, he suspected that computers would be the future and he wanted to be in on the ground floor. His manager in the shop, was a guy called Jeffery Price. Tommy would never have chosen him as a friend, he was studious, had little personality and rarely spoke unless he had to.
Late in 1983, Tommy visited the shop unannounced as was always his way, he liked to keep all his managers on their toes and unannounced visits was a good way. Jeff, as Tommy liked to call him as he knew it wound him up, was dealing with an upset customer, who had returned to the shop with a computer he had bought earlier in the week.
"It just doesn't bloody work" the customer said, raising his voice.
"You probably don't know how to use it" came the terse reply. 'Not a great way to speak to a customer' thought Tommy. "This is a Galvian SC, it is top of the range, not something for an amateur," added Jeff
Also in the shop, was a skinny teenager who was browsing the shelves, looking at each computer with great concentration. Before anyone could say anything else he piped up with, "you probably installed the drives incorrectly. The sequence for the Galvian is different to other computers."
"Shut up you and get out anyway. You never buy anything. You're just keeping warm in here."

"Right, everybody just calm down" said Tommy, "I'm sorry sir what's your name?"

"Trimble, Arthur Trimble"

"Jeff, have we got Mr Trimble's phone number on file?"

"Yes" replied Jeff, surly.

"Mr Trimble, I am Tommy Flounders, I own this shop. Would it be alright if we were to keep this computer overnight? If it can't be fixed, I will either purchase you an upgrade for no extra cost or refund you every penny you have paid."

"Tommy Flounders, yes, I have heard of you, I hear you are an honest man. Tomorrow morning is fine, if I have your word Mr Flounders."

As soon as Mr Trimble left, Tommy turned to the young man who had spoken up earlier, "and what's your name son?"

"Terry Begley, Mr Flounders."

"Wait a minute. Would your mum happened to be called Julie?"

"Yes sir."

"OK then, now come into the back with me 'n' Jeff and let's see if you know what you are talking about."

"The problem with the Galvian SC" began Terry, "is that the disc's that were supplied with it have been issued in the wrong order. Disc 4 should be loaded onto the computer between disc 2 and 3. Doing them in the order they were supplied, drains memory and CPU, which slows the computer down."

"And you know this how?" said Jeff.

"I read it. I buy every computer magazine I can find and if I have no money, I pinch them."

"How long will it take you to sort this out Jeff?" asked Tommy.

"Four or five hours to wipe the hard drive and three to install the disks again, if you want to take the word of this child."
"You can wipe the drive quicker if you want to, I know a way. It should be done in less than an hour. Tell you what Mr Flounders, let me take it home, with the disks and I will have it ready for you to collect in the morning at 8 o'clock. Jeff should be able to check the performance in twenty minutes or so."
"Jeff, do we have a spare computer, if Terry here isn't the man he claims he is?"
"Yes," said Jeff through gritted teeth, clearly put out with what had transpired.
"Right, meet me here at 08:30 tomorrow. I will drop Terry off now, with the computer and we'll see how he gets on in the morning."
Terry, beaming, collected the master disks from Jeff and picked up the computer, heading out to Tommy's car.
"Can you bring the monitor Mr Flounders?"
"Yes son and call me Tommy"
"You and your mum still over on the West View?" he asked Terry, as he settled into the car.
"Yes Mr Flounders. How did you know that?"
"Oh, I knew your mum and her dad, a few years ago."
"Me grandad passed away last year Mr Flounders."
"Call me Tommy son and I am sorry about that."
Fifteen minutes later, Terry led Tommy back into the house he had last visited 4 years ago, and to Tommy's delight, it still smelt the same.
"Is that you Terry?" his mum called out.
"Yes mum," he said, as he walked into the living room.
Julie Begley looked up, jumped up, flattened her skirt with her hands then ran one through her hair whilst at the same time saying,

"Oh, Mr Flounders!" quickly followed by, "Terry what have you been up to, and what is that?" pointing at the computer that Terry had just sat on the folding table, that nestled one wall.
"It's ok Miss Begley," said Tommy. "Terry happened to be in one of my shops and we got talking about computers. I want to see if he is as good as he says he is and understand how he knows so much."
"Well I can tell you how he knows so much," said his mum. "He goes through to Newcastle every Saturday and comes back with arms full of computer magazines, that are worth far more than he leaves with in his pocket, that's for sure." Throwing Terry a daggers look.
"I've told you mum," said Terry. "I get a discount."
"Right well. I tell you what," Tommy intervened, sensing a domestic hurtling towards him. "If Terry does a good job with this computer, and if you are in agreement Miss Begley, I will give Terry a Saturday job and a few hours during the week, if it doesn't interrupt his schooling. In payment, I will arrange for every magazine he buys, to be subscribed to my shop for him, as part of the deal."
Terry beamed. "Really Mr Flounders?"
"Only if your mum agrees, and if of course, you can fix this computer."
"Please call me Julie and yes, as long as your school work doesn't suffer Terry."
"No chance of that mum, I know more than the lecturers. I do computer studies Mr Flounders. It's a brand new course 'n' we got all sorts of dummies trying to teach us it."
"You work for me now son and I have already asked you, to call me Tommy. Now make sure that," he nodded towards the computer, "is fixed and ready for me to collect tomorrow at 8 o'clock ok?"
"Yes Tommy."

"Well, if you will excuse me Miss Begley, I will be on my way."

"Please call me Julie, Mr Flounders. Come let me see you out."

"In that case," he said as they left the living room, "you must call me Tommy."

"Are you sure I can't make you a cup of tea Tommy, it will only take a minute?"

"I would love to Julie but I have a prior appointment. Another time maybe?"

Tommy could see that Julie looked disappointed and felt bad about that, but he was meeting a local councillor and needed to be on time.

"Yes sure, Mr Flounders."

"It's Tommy remember, and trust me, I will hold you to this cup of tea."

Julie looked a little happier as Tommy left, she unconsciously pulled at a lock of hair, as he closed the front garden gate behind him.

Tommy jumped into his car, feeling happier than he had in a long time, without knowing why.

The following morning, he arrived at 07:55. He was going to wait until 08:00 but as soon as he had parked, Terry opened the door with the computer in his hands and an ASDA bag that contained the discs.

"All done Tommy," he said, almost cockily. "See if happy Jeff can find anything wrong with that?"

"Thank you, Terry, but remember, happy Jeff runs that store for me. So he will be your boss and until he tells you different, he is Mr Price."

Suitably reprimanded, Terry said, "sorry Tommy and yes, I will remember. I will just get you the monitor and you can be on your way."

"Right, I will see you on Saturday at 9 sharp, at the shop. Ok?"

"Aint you going to have it checked first?" Terry asked.
"If it aint good son, you will see me before then, for sure." There was just a hint of menace in Tommy's voice, enough to remind Terry of their business relationship.

Terry, a smile spreading across his face said "see you Saturday then," he turned and went back in, to collect the monitor.

An hour later, Jeff had checked out the computer and, despite his moans and groans, had confirmed that it was now running better than ever.

Three hours later, a delighted Arthur Trimble was shaking Tommy's hand in the shop, over the moon with the speed of the computer. As he shook Tommy's hand, he looked pointedly at Jeff.

"You should learn from this son," he said, "this is how a business should be run. I was right when I said it was no good and it took your manager to resolve it. He did your job," and with that, he turned on his heels and left the shop.

"He's right you know Jeff," said Tommy "I know fuck all about computers but even I could see it wasn't right but the big issue, was how you spoke to him. You told him he did not know what he was doing and called him an amateur. He had bought the top of the range computer from us and you were doing your very best to lose his business."

"It wasn't that. It's just"

"Jeff shut up and let me finish. You are one of the most knowledgeable people in the town, when it comes to computers but you were wrong. You refused to admit you were wrong and you refused to admit there may be an issue, with a product we had sold.

Now part of what you did, is my responsibility. You run this shop five and a half days a week, with no support.

That changes this Saturday. On Saturday, we will have a new employee. It's Terry Begley. He will come in here at 9am, I will be here to meet him. His role will be to clear up the back room of part built and exchange computers, that are building up, and to assist you in any way that you ask. You are the manager of this shop Jeff and you have to utilise every tool you have available, Terry will be a tool for you to utilise. Like it or not, he fixed something, you said wasn't broken. He had knowledge you didn't. But that doesn't make him more valuable than you. You are the manager, so manage and use him. If you don't know, ask him. If he steps out of line, tell me and I will deal with him. And for fucks sake, never ever speak to a customer like that again. Is there anything I have just said that you don't understand Jeff? Anything that you need me to clarify?"

"No Tommy."

"Good stuff. I will see you Saturday and remember, I made you manager of this shop because I trust you."

On Saturday morning, Tommy arrived at the shop at 08:30, Jeff was already in. As was Terry, who was elbows deep on a makeshift work bench, with the side off a computer and a grin on his face.

"This is fanfuckingtastic Tommy. All of these to fix. Once these are done, can I start on those?" he nodded to a row of boxes of new computers, that needed software installing.

"One step at a time son. Here," Tommy chucked a note pad, followed by a pen, at Terry "write down the name of every magazine you need and I will walk down to Smith's. I'll arrange for them to be ordered and delivered here."

"All of them?"

"Yes, Terry. All of them."

Five minutes later, Tommy had a list of magazines from Terry. He quickly scanned down them. All were monthly's and, nearly all Terry had marked up as American imports. The bottom of the list brought a smile to Tommy's face.

"Bacon buttie Terry," said Tommy, "an unusual name for a magazine."

"Yeah, I know, it's a proper hot one," he said, grinning.

Twenty minutes later Tommy, Jeff and Terry had mugs of tea and bacon butties in hand. Even Jeff seemed to warm to Terry's enthusiasm.

Forty minutes after that, Tommy left the shop, quietly confident that Terry would be an asset for the business and that he and Jeff might actually work well together. 'Chalk and cheese,' he thought to himself. Although he was confident, he made it a regular occurrence, that first thing Saturday morning he would arrive with bacon sandwiches for the three of them. They would review what Terry had achieved the previous week, he had Jeff lead the review, which achieved 2 things. Firstly, Jeff confirmed that Terry was doing a good job for them and secondly, that Jeff was the shop manager. Tommy had torn a strip off him and he wanted Jeff to feel secure in his role.

Six weeks later, Terry was working three afternoons a week and Saturday mornings. Every part exchange computer was now out on display, for sale again and every display model computer had been set up and was in place. Sales were up, Jeff was less stressed, and the two of them grumbled affectionately at each other, like an old pair of fishwives.

People were visiting the shop from Middlesbrough, Sunderland and Newcastle, as word quickly spread about the level of service and expertise, that was available at Flounders Computers. Terry became an

integral part of the business. He had an enquiring mind and could easily translate what he read in books, into physical actions. His love of computers was clear to see. He spent time with customers, helping them understand how to better utilise their purchases.
Tommy called on Terry and his mum, Julie, one May evening.
"Is it all right if I come in?" he asked Julie, who answered the door.
"Of course it is Mr Flounders, I mean Tommy, come on in."
Terry was sat in the living room, his head buried in a computer magazine. He jumped up when Tommy and Julie walked in.
"Tommy, is everything alright?" he asked.
"I just popped over, to make sure you were revising for your exam Terry. You don't want to fail at the last hurdle now, do you?"
Terry, as always, beamed when he spoke. "No worries there. I have forgot more than the course has taught me."
"Cocky little bugger," said his mum.
"As long as you are sure son," said Tommy. "After all, you will need this qualification, for me to be able to offer you full time employment. If that's all right with you Julie?"
"Yes!" shouted Terry, punching the air, cutting off Julie's answer, which was also yes but a lot more reserved.
"It's five and a half days a week Terry and I will start you on £150 per week. Free magazines and a bonus scheme linked to the shop's profits."
"I expect you to pay your mum a decent amount of keep each week, after all she has had to put up with you all of these years."
"No problems there Tommy, honest."

"Good. Now, did you mention a cup of tea last time I was here Julie?"

"Oh my god Tommy, I am so sorry." Julie looked horror struck that Tommy had to ask.

Tommy couldn't help but laugh and the next hour was spent laughing and joking with the Begley's. It was, Tommy thought when he reflected on it, one of the best hours he had spent in a long time.

32

Tommy's bookmaker's shops had gone from strength to strength, under Jacko's close management. So much so, that Tommy had given Jacko responsibility for the retail side of his businesses, allowing Tommy to concentrate on new business and investments.

Tommy still caught up with Gary Tanners, occasionally, to compare notes and seek mutual opportunities. Whilst they rarely had joint ventures, those that they did, were very lucrative. Gary had gained a few pounds and was as content as any man Tommy knew.

Tommy and Jacko continued to shoot at Catterick, both using the pistol and rifle ranges. After shooting, Tommy would sit and sip a whiskey at the bar, allowing Jacko to catch up with his old buddies around a table for an hour. After one such occasion, Jacko joined Tommy at the bar.

"Do you need a container full of TVs by any chance?"

"Why's that?" asked Tommy.

"We have a man who shoots here regularly, who delivers them up North from Felixstowe Docks. He needs a couple of hundred quid and is happy to take a bang on the bonce to get it."

Tommy had no need to take risks in his life. He was comparatively cash rich. He had thriving businesses, was well respected in the town and had never been arrested in his life. But he missed the thrill of the life he once led, as a gangster and listening to Omar's story's once a week. In short, he was exceptionally bored and this sounded like it could be a simple little number and add some excitement to his life.

"When?" he asked Jacko.

"He does a run about once a month, maybe every 6 weeks or so. He did one 3 weeks ago, so maybe next week or the week after."

"Too soon for us to plan it. Taking the lorry is fine, moving the stuff is a different matter but I have an idea."
"Tell your man we will be in touch. How often does he come here?"
"Once a week, on a Saturday. If he isn't working or if he is on a run and can park up."
"Ok leave it with me and I will get back to both of you."
The following Monday, Tommy spent an hour in Middlesbrough central library, where they stocked all of the UK's telephone directories. There were three Peter Scott's in the directory, in and around Tranmere and a further nine in Liverpool, in general. On the second number, Tommy got lucky.
"Pete, it's Tommy Flounders. How are you doing buddy?" Tommy was genuinely pleased to hear Pete's voice again.
Pete sounded hesitant on the phone. He had left the gang life behind him, when he left Hartlepool and wanted no part of it now. He worked as a caretaker for a local school and did a little bit of decorating, during his days off.
"Listen Pete, could you do me a favour? I need to make contact with one of the Liverpool guys, to see if we could do a little business together. I will give you a number and I will be by the phone Monday to Friday from 5pm to 7, all of next week. Would you do that for me buddy?"
"That's it, Tommy?" said Pete. "I want no involvement whatsoever."
"I know Pete and I promise if all goes to plan, I will drop a healthy drink off for you, if you want one."
"Yeah, but not here Tommy, my missus would have kittens."
"No worries buddy. I will be in touch."

The following Tuesday at 5pm on the dot, the phone rang and the harsh nasal tones of a scouse accent filled Tommy's ear.
"What?"
"I have some TV's coming my way, I wondered if you would like to meet to discuss?"
"Pete said you were the young lad that came with our Billy, all those years ago. Is that right?"
"Yeah that's me, although not so young now."
"Mersey Park tomorrow at 3. Wander around the pond, I will find you" and with that he hung up. Despite being just a little pissed off with the Scouse twat's attitude, Tommy was pleased that the phone call was kept to a minimum. The choice of venue suited him better than a rundown bar, that most villains tended to use. Out in the open meant safer.
The following day Tommy was feeding the ducks, when a guy he vaguely recognised, wandered over.
"What are we talking about then?"
"TV's. A fucking lorry load." Tommy went on to tell his new contact, 'Alby,' that he had an inside man and could get a shedload of Colour TV's, fresh from the docks. Although he had somewhere to store them, he did not have the network to move them on. Getting rid of them two or three at a time did not appeal to him, nor did involving the Turks, who were now even more heavily into drugs and prostitution.
"So, I need someone who will give me a fair price and be able to take them, on a few days' notice. A colour set is around £250 these days, so how about £100 per unit?"
They two guys haggled a bit and agreed a price of £75 per set. Nothing upfront, cash on delivery. The Scousers would probably move them on for £125, so it was a fair compromise.

"I see this as a test for both of us." said Tommy. I have a network of drivers that carry all sorts of goods. If this goes well, I can pretty much get you a lorry of something, every couple of weeks."
The guys shook hands on the deal and walked away, in opposite directions.
Tommy was shocked to see Pete, when he met him at a local boozer. He had aged and seem to have shrunk in stature. He was too polite to ask out right, so simply said "how's things Pete?" handing over the £50 drink, he had promised him.
"I got the cancer Tommy. Doc said it's 50/50, so this will come in handy, thank you." Tommy immediately doubled it and instinctively wrapped his arms around the smaller older man. "Keep fighting buddy and call me if you need me."

33

The plan was a simple one. The vehicle would be lifted at Doncaster, driven to a warehouse in Liverpool and then dumped in a truck stop, just outside Manchester. The driver would tell police that he was hit over the head, bound and gagged, kept for 10 hours and then let go on a country lane. He would take a bit of a slapping, to make it realistic.
Including Tommy, Jacko and the driver, one other man was involved. The driver would get £1000, the substitute driver £750, with Tommy and Jacko splitting the rest. The vehicle contained 26 pallets of 6 TV's each nearly £12k in total. A nice little pay day. The driver was not happy about waiting for the money for a month but Tommy explained that this was the only way it would work. If the driver came into cash straight away, the bizzies might just catch wind of it and they would put a whole load of pressure on him. The driver suspected that Tommy was going to rip him off, but Jacko vouched for him and the fact all three used the same shooting range, was enough to convince him that Tommy was worth a gamble.
"After all," said Jacko, "right now you are guaranteed nothing. Trust us and you are a grand up."
On the day, everything went like clockwork. Jacko dropped off the substitute driver, collected the original one and drove out to a country lane, where he hit him hard on the back of his head. Chuckling, he apologised, as the man swore blind that Jacko had hit him too hard.
"Fucks sake, you cunt, you trying to kill me?"
"It's got to look convincing" he said, over the drivers' complaints. After a visit to a small caff, on the edge of Leeds, they killed time until Jacko dropped him off, at a

layby on the A1, where he had to flag down someone to get help.
In the meantime, Tommy shadowed the lorry to the warehouse and met Alby just inside. Within minutes, the vehicle was unloaded.
"I guess this is the bit you're most worried about, ey Tommy?"
"Nah" came the reply. "I know your good for it and I know you want more of this."
Alby grinned, took Tommy to an office.
"£11700 in this bag. Do you want to count it?"
"Not here buddy but I will be, for sure."
Tommy knew he could not show weakness, although felt that Alby was genuine enough.
"Yeah, I would too. If I were you." came the reply.
Alby gave Tommy a scrap of paper, with a number on.
"Call me when you have something else. Take care fella."
An hour after that, Tommy and the substitute driver left the lorry, just outside of Manchester and headed back up North.
Afterwards, Tommy and Jacko had a couple of beers, in the yard. Tommy had replaced the old portacabin with a newer, better equipped one. He had also refurbished the restroom area for the lads and installed a shower. Lastly, he had put a caravan on site that he could use to kip in, if ever the need came.
"That was a doddle," said Jacko.
'And it was,' thought Tommy, lying in the dirt waiting for 7am to roll around. Those were the easy days, no CCTV, no VNPR, no mobile phones, no forensics and DNA. All that a man needed was a plan and the courage to carry it out. Tommy had both.

34

The next time Tommy saw Alby was at the funeral of Pete. It was just 5 weeks after the TV sets had been dropped off, at Alby's warehouse. They both paid their respects to Pete's wife at the wake. They both discreetly passed her an envelope, the contents of which would more than take care of the funeral, and then sat away from the crowd at a quiet table, in the noisy bar.
"Lot of space in my warehouse Tommy" began Alby.
"What would you like to fill it with?" asked Tommy.
"Designer gear, trainers, shell suits, Armani, Ralph Lauren, Calvin Klein. Anything like that mate."
"I will see what I can do."
In the end, a smaller vehicle mainly Reebok and Adidas, was the next drop. Again, everything went smoothly. Tommy and Jacko never used the same delivery driver twice, although they always used the same substitute driver. Andrew Leeson was as sound as a pound. Jacko had known him for years, although he would bend the law to make a bob, he was straight up and down with his friends. Tommy and Jacko took a back seat when it came to arranging everything. The drivers never knew who was funding the robberies. Safety, was always Tommy's watch word. He and Jacko planned and checked. Always paying drivers a month or so after the robbery and always in cash.
In January 1984, Alby arranged a trip up to Hartlepool, which was the first time any meet had happened away from Merseyside. They met at the portacabin, in Tommy's scrap yard. Alby had driven across from the North West by himself and Tommy was also alone. After handshakes and a brew was made, they got down to business.

Alby explained that he had a problem, with a rival gang. The gang in question, was in fact, several smaller gangs. Mainly lads in their late teens and early 20's.
Unusually, rather than clashing with each other over territory or imagined slights, they actually divvied out responsibility and income. With a small group from different post codes meeting regularly, to sort out any issues and share out money and responsibilities, Alby explained. They were ruthless and relied on intimidation and extreme violence to run their whores, sell their drugs, blag whatever they wanted and expand into new businesses. This was the problem, Alby ran a number of whore houses and 5 of them had been shut down. Two burnt to the ground and three trashed so badly, punters would never return. The coppers Alby paid off, couldn't do anything about it. Any soldier that was caught, either got off with a good brief or kept silent and did his time. Alby was being squeezed.
He has a good mob himself but not killers, well not many of them, which brought Alby to his point.
"Do you know anyone who could do a number of hits for me? Pretty much at the same time."
Tommy was hesitant but he liked Alby. He always seemed the decent type.
"I might," he said, "but the guy's I work with, plan and plan again, and won't come cheap."
"I have £40K and some intel, but your guys would need to gather the rest. If I can make it look like inter gang feuding, the cops won't look too hard. It will be case closed in days, as long as me and my team are in the clear, and have alibis, it's a done deal."
Tommy asked what sort of window Alby was talking about for the hits? Alby wanted to take at least three, if not four, of the leaders out, all over one night.

"They will disintegrate into small factions," he explained "fighting each other. If I do it, one at a time, they will lock down. It could take months. I can take care of two of them myself, if you can arrange to take care of the other two.
They always meet Friday night, in a rundown pub in Toxteth, then they go out clubbing. I want to get them after the club, either when they go home or when they turn up at their gaffs the next day. They mostly don't surface until Saturday afternoon. If we hit them last thing Friday, we should get all four of them before word gets out, with a bit of luck."
"Before we start talking about dates Alby, give me the name and addresses of the two you want me to deal with. I will arrange for a little surveillance, next week, and get back to you after that."
"Be quick Tommy. These guys are really hurting me."
"Alby, I will be safe, not quick. However long we need, we need. I have to arrange the guys and the weapons, if we go ahead. So, while I do this, push the fuck back. Show them you are good for a fight, if they want one."
The following Friday, Jacko and Andrew Leeson sat outside the flats where 'Tocker,' one of the two marks lived. Tommy and another soldier, that Jacko had served with, Pudding Smithies ghosting the second mark 'Smithy.'
All three of the ex-service men, had served in Northern Ireland and were well versed in street warfare.
Saturday morning, they met for breakfast and a de-brief. Jacko for once taking the lead, not Tommy.
"Tocker arrived back at 3:30am. He was pissed. We could have pushed him over. He was dropped by some geezer in an AUDI turbo. He had to walk across a pavement, then into the flats. No one was with him, I could have took him then."

Tommy told a similar story. His mark 'Smithy,' arrived home at 2:55. He was sober and driving himself, a space had been left outside his house on a terraced street. No doubt everyone was intimidated on the street and left him a spot, right outside his door. But he parks with the driver's door to the road and had to walk around the car, to get to his door, it was locked. So, there is time but it is tight."

The army guys were confident it could be done. The marks lived some miles from each other. Even if the cops were quick to the scene of the first killing, they wouldn't have any reason to suspect another might be about to take place, and more deaths in a short period of time, would only add to the confusion.

Andrew Leeson and Pudding Smithies then headed back up North, in Jacko's car.

"No fucking speeding and park it at the barracks," said Jacko adding, "make sure you book the fucker in. I don't want it blowing up. As a precaution. Ok?"

Pudding Smithies grinned.

"Fuck me Jacko, you were the sergeant, we're grunts. We aint going to fuck up, that's above our grade."

Tommy and Jacko then met with Alby, in his warehouse.

"OK Alby, we are pretty sure we can do this, with no repercussions. I know you are keen to make this happen, as soon as possible but we do have to make sure we are good to go and have contingencies, should we need them. Not next Friday but the Friday afterwards, I will come back with a firm date. It will be done within 5 weeks from today. How does that sound?"

"I don't like to have to fucking wait. These guys are squeezing me. Are you sure you will be good for 5 weeks?"

"You have my word."

"Fair enough fella. See you soon."

On the drive up North, Jacko said to Tommy, "Something's not right about this. I can't put me finger on it but I have an itch, and I trust my itch with my life."
"Do you want to pull out?" asked Tommy, "I will pull the plug, if you want to."
"Nah, but I want to go back for a couple of days next week and do another recce. Something stinks and I aim to find out what."
The following Monday, Jacko and Pudding Smithies, drove back across to Liverpool in two separate cars. On Friday, they returned to Hartlepool. Jacko arranged to meet with Tommy at the yard.
"Sorry pal," said Jacko, " this cunt Alby, has had you over." Tommy felt a chill run down his spine.
"Tell me everything buddy."
"First off, Tocker, he runs a gang pretty much as Alby has told you. He has a crew running around the area just outside of the docks, but they look like bottom feeders. Thieves and pushers, not the gangsters that Alby has been talking about. We could hit him easily enough but it seems a bit extreme. He's probably caused Alby some low level noise but we are talking execution, for theft! The problem lies with the second mark Smithy. He's clean Tommy. He boxes at a local amateur club and he's serving an apprenticeship as an electrician. He's a face but not a bad lad and he's tomming Alby's daughter, Laura."
Tommy let the facts sink in.
"So, Alby wants us to hit a low level gang leader and a clean civvy, who is pretty much a good lad, just because his daughter is getting her bones jumped on, by him."
"Yeah, maybe he don't like blacks Tommy. Let's face it, I wouldn't want no half casts in the family, but he's using you mate. The coppers would be all over his killing. We could do it, and do it clean, but it don't make sense. It

wouldn't be seen as gang on gang, and you can guarantee Alby will be seen somewhere, miles from Liverpool, a cast iron alibi."

"Fuck that!" said Tommy," I aint about to start killing innocent kids, just for that twat or any other fucker, come to think of it. Ok, it's plan B then, and if you're wondering what plan B is, well here's what we are about to do."

35

A week later Tommy, Alby and Jacko sat down in Alby's office.
"Alright Tommy everything good, when are you doing it?"
"You need to see these first Alby," said Tommy. passing a manilla A4 envelope to Alby. Inside there were a series of photographs. The first 4 were of Alby's daughter Laura and Smithy her boyfriend, who Alby wanted killing. "You forgot to mention to us that Smithy here, who by the way has no affinity to any gang activity, is seeing your daughter. Fuck sake Alby. He goes to college and is a rising star in the amateur boxing ranks, he's exactly what I was when I was his age. The police will be all over this. You have taken me for a mug fella. The next 12 pictures are of you entering some of your whore houses and also meeting with your mistress in the flat you own. For future reference, you need to learn how to close the curtains properly, if you don't want to be caught getting your cock sucked by a schoolgirl."
"She's fucking legit, she's sixteen," snarled Alby.
"That's as maybe," said Jacko, "but she's still a schoolgirl, and as it happens is still in her uniform as you feed her your cock."
"You will also find an itinerary of names, dates, addresses. There are some people here, who would not like this and their association to you to become public. All except, of course, Bob Jones."
"Who?" Asked Alby.
"He works for the Liverpool Echo Alby. Young, enthusiastic and idealist. I know he would love to go to press with this."
Alby shot out of his seat "are you fucking trying to blackmail me you cunts I could have you killed right here and right now."

"Do you know what Alby, I'm not sure you could but just in case, if we don't leave in 20 minutes, the police will receive an anonymous phone call saying there is a little bit of mischief going on here. At the same time, a copy of everything I have given you, will be dropped off at the Liverpool Echo marked FAO Bob Jones. So sit the fuck down and shut the fuck up."
Alby paced the room, his face red, his hands flexing.
"Enough of the fucking theatre, for fucks sake," said Jacko. "We aint fucking impressed. Now do yourself a favour and sit the fuck down." Alby sat.
"So Alby," Tommy began, "today marks the end of our association, in so much as we will never do business again. However, we will be keeping an eye on Smithy and if he comes to any harm. this fucking lot will be getting published. You fed me a total line, in order for us to hit 2 young men. One of whom needs a kicking and reminding where not to pilfer from. The other needs nothing at all, other than to watch his back around his future father-in-law and you wanted me to off them for you, you spineless cunt. Now compensation."
"What!" roared Alby, "you are off your fucking trolley. You aint getting anything mate"
"Compensation Alby" said Tommy, ignoring Alby's outburst. "We agreed £40K to kill gangsters. You have not provided us with any gangsters, so we will take the 20K you have here for us now and call it quits."
"The fuck you will," snarled Alby.
"Alby, think for a fucking minute, you dumb cunt. You have tried to mug me over and you have been found out. I have put down in front of you an envelope that will ruin you, cause your family to break up. Your daughter will know her Father wanted her boyfriend killed. You would certainly go to jail and if any of the named men on here have anything to do with it, you wouldn't get out alive. Be

fucking grateful I only want £20k. Now I know you have it, as it was going to be the deposit you handed over today. So go fucking get it.
It's a life lesson. When you do what you do here, on Merseyside, you may feel like you are invincible. A face, who knows maybe one day one of the biggest faces, but you made a mistake. You know me, you know how I work, how I plan, how I check and still you tried to mug me. It has cost you our partnership and unless you do exactly as I say, it will cost you everything, your wife, your daughter, your liberty. Now go get the money, we have only 10 minutes left."
Alby went to a filing cabinet and threw a small suitcase, at the feet of Tommy.
"This aint fucking over, you Northern bastard."
"Alby, it is over because if anything happens to me, to Jacko, to any of our associates or your daughter's boyfriend, everything we have shown you goes to press. Now grow up and move on, and never reach out to me again."
With that, Tommy and Jacko stood and left.
As they drove off, two further cars moved out and shadowed them, all the way back to Hartlepool. It pays to be careful.
Tommy passed Jacko the £20k.
"Share this out buddy. I suggest ten for you and five each for Pudding and Andrew."
"What about you?" asked Jacko. "Nothing for me pal. I made a mistake. Alby is the third man I have trusted, that has let me down. The other two I killed, with my bare hands. He's fucking lucky he aint the third, but that money is tainted and I don't want it."

36

In January 1985, Tommy began to retail mobile phones, along with the computers he sold. This arm of his business had gone from strength to strength, with Jeff and Terry now having a team of seven people working for them. Two on the shop floor, which was now three times the space of the old shop they had moved from. They now had a prime position, overlooking the central square, in the Middleton Grange shopping centre. The remainder of the team worked for Terry, in the backroom building up and repairing computers, along with visiting clients and installing computers into their work places. Terry had quickly established himself as an expert. He had almost a Midas touch with technology, advising Tommy to invest in licences to retail Microsoft office. He was that enthusiastic and knowledgeable, that on his advice Tommy had bought himself, Jacko, Terry and Jeff shares in Microsoft, in March of the following year.
Jeff and Terry were now firm friends. Terry floated between the shop and the backroom, helping the sales team with the more technical questions and keeping an eye on his staff of young techies, that like him all had a natural aptitude rather than an academic background, although all were put through college by Tommy. Tommy felt a real affinity for Terry. 'There's something about that kid,' he thought one day, 'I don't know what it is but I need to keep him close.'
Jeff was now also more valued by Tommy. It had turned out that he had a very dry, wicked sense of humour. He often said something, in his prissy high pitched voice, that made Tommy laugh out loud. Since Terry had joined the business, Jeff had become much more relaxed and had developed a sales manner that made almost

everyone he served look at him like their favourite old uncle, even if he was younger than his customer.
Tommy felt sure that his business future would lay with computers. He had never seen anything develop as quickly and revolutionary as computer technology. He could not think of any business that could not be enhanced by the ever improving world of computer science.

Every couple of years, Tommy reviewed all of his businesses and decided what, if any, changes he had to make to the medium and long term strategy. In 1986, he decided with Jacko, that it was about time to let the bookmakers go. Profits were still good although the trend was down. They were labour intensive and time consuming. A local company, Jack Lithgo Turf Accountants, had made an approach to buy the business and goodwill. He knew that this would mean at least six of the bookies closing, as they were in direct conflict with a Jack Lithgo shop, but business was business and the offer was as favourable as Tommy could ever see them getting.

Tommy also had other plans for Jacko, in a new business, that would make Jacko a full partner.

37

In September 1986, just after the sale of the bookmakers, Titanium security was established. The premises were in an administration unit on the Park View Industrial Estate. The main part of the business would be providing site security, including, on site security personnel, site patrols and drive by audits, along with installation and maintenance of CCTV. They had a constant line of ex-soldiers seeking jobs in civvy street and the discipline of 12 hour security shifts suited an ex-serviceman perfectly. Customers also liked the idea of security guards that could handle themselves.

The remaining part of the business being Computer network protection, which worked hand in hand with the supply and installation packages, that his shop offered to companies in the area.

Terry was to front this up and had his salary almost doubled, from that he was earning in the shop, whilst Tommy and Jacko would take dividends from the business periodically, if profits were in line with the forecast. The computer arm of the business had two main revenue streams. Firstly, Security Awareness classes, either at the customer's premises or onsite at Titanium Security. The classes identified areas of possible concern and strategies to minimise the risk. This was aimed at business directors and their IT team. The second stream of the business, was customer visits, which would involve Terry and maybe one of his backroom boys, checking the integrity of a business network, identifying opportunities to improve networking and, if the customer agreed, establishing the protocols for this work.

Tommy and Jacko had thought about having a branch offering door work for nightclubs and pubs, but there was

a lot of competition, as it normally went hand in hand with selling drugs and Tommy didn't want to step back into that world. A little ducking and diving was fine but drugs were trouble. Whilst the rewards were high so were the risks.
Tommy would still dip his toe into the murky waters of criminal activity but he was very cautious when he did so, therefore door work was left alone.
The computer shop continued to flourish. Jeff now had a lad from Newcastle, known as Eggy, heading up the back room staff. Whilst he did not have the charm and character of Terry, he was more than competent and could speak in layman's terms along with being fluent in geek, as Tommy would comment, if he heard two techies discussing a problem.
Most of the backroom boys now worked in a purpose built workshop, that was housed at the Titanium security unit. The workshop featured clean areas, static reduction systems along with anti-contamination protocols. It had cost Tommy an arm and a leg to establish, but when corporate clients were entertained in a bid to win business, it was always one of the first places Tommy or Jacko headed to. It reeked of cutting edge technology and with its high intensity lights, desk tools and magnifying glasses, for close soldering work, it looked very high tech and impressive.
The space that had been saved in the shop, had been turned over to video consoles and their games.
Despite the fact, every Saturday it became full of kids with little in their pockets and, given the chance, light fingers. It was exceptionally lucrative with mum's 'n' dads being dragged in, frequently to buy the new Sega or Nintendo game.

38

Terry's mum, Julie, now worked full time as a receptionist at Titanium security. She had an air of vulnerability, a quiet charm about her that seemed to make just about everyone she met, like her. She was also very good at what she did. For Jacko, she was great sport too.
"When are you going to grow some balls and ask her out?" He would rip into Tommy, at every opportunity. "Everyone can see you fancy her and here you are sat upstairs like a little schoolboy, trying to build up the courage to ask her on a date. Ask her out you fucking dummy."
"I will fucking knock you out, if you don't change the subject, you prat," Tommy growled in reply.
Tommy knew that Jacko was right, he really did fancy Julie Begley. He had since the first time he had met her but it was complicated. He was a free spirit. She wasn't a date and a shag kind of girl. Terry was thriving in the business, Julie was exceptionally competent and he didn't want to blow it all, by starting a relationship with her. So he spent as much time with her as he could, without it becoming too obvious.
One day in the spring of 1987, Tommy sat down to have lunch with Julie in the canteen. They always enjoyed each other's company, rarely talking about work but always filled in their lunch breaks chatting about anything that came to mind, both very comfortable with each other.
"Can I ask you a personal question?" asked Julie, "and I do want an honest answer, Tommy."
"Sure, go ahead," said Tommy.
"What's wrong with me? We always have fun together. We like each other and you never ask me out. Do I smell

or have I done something to offend you? Tommy Flounders, I want a date." Then she went bright red and looked down.
Tommy's stomach flipped.
"Julie," he said, "I would like nothing better but I am really not sure I am the right guy for you. I like you so much, I just don't want to screw things up between us."
"Well, if you don't pick me up Friday night at 7.30, you bloody will have!" She stood, picked up her sandwich box and walked out of the canteen, her hips swinging in a way that had always had Tommy's attention.
The next three days dragged for Tommy. Julie left the office for her lunch. Tommy had little chance to talk to her and when he did, she was strictly professional.
He had confided in Jacko, who thought the whole thing was exceptionally amusing.
 "Aw Tommy, are you nervous?" teased Jacko, "what happened to the man about town. Wine, dine, bang and bye? Don't tell me you are falling in love."
"Fuck off you twat, before I sack you," rumbled Tommy, half serious.
Friday 7.30 arrived, as did Tommy at Julie's door. He had actually been parked around the corner for 20 minutes, leaving his house early, in order to make sure he was not late. Dressed in a smart casual combination of jacket, shirt, slacks and Italian loafers. He knocked on the door and waited, and waited, for what seemed like an age but was actually less than 30 seconds.
"Hello handsome" said Julie, she looked a picture. She had on an oversized shirt, hanging down over light blue coloured Levi jeans with flat sandals, nothing expensive or sophisticated, but she took Tommy's breath away.
"You look stunning" he said.

"I know" she replied, showing confidence Tommy had never imagined she had. "You look quite dashing yourself," she added.

He walked her to his Golf GTI, which was one of the luxuries he allowed himself, as his businesses and wealth had grown. The night passed in an instant. They had a meal at Elwick before a last drink at the Greensides pub, which was outside of the town centre but very trendy. Tommy stuck to fruit juices, whilst Julie had wine spritzers. They never stopped talking and loved each other's company.

They arrived back at Julie's just after eleven.

"Terry is out tonight," she said. "Would you like to come in for a night cap?"

Ten minutes later, coffee at their feet, they sat close together on Julie's sofa.

"Tommy," she said "I have had a lovely evening. Everything I had imagined it would be and more. I think I have fancied you since you first walked into my house, when my dad was here, all those years ago. The trouble is, so do half the women in Hartlepool and if some of what I hear is true, you have bedded most of them. I'm not that kind of girl Tommy. I have had a wonderful night and would love to do it again, but I'm not a one-night stand. So, if you would like to date me, you need to promise me that you will only date me. I'm not about to become another notch on your bed post."

"How about lunch on Sunday then" Tommy replied, and in an instant they became a couple.

39

Life was good for Tommy. In 1987, he was 37 years old, dating a girl that he had liked for years. His businesses were flourishing. He had a lovely home and was mortgage free. The cash he had invested was doing well for him. If he chose to, he could have sold up then and never have had to work again.
Jacko had really found his niche in the security business. His Army background suited him well. He had a canny knack of being able to read people and altered his sales pitch to suit. Most employers were happy to take on ex-service men, they had a reputation of honesty and were prepared to put in long hours.
The men Jacko chose, he knew to be reliable and very loyal. Loyal to him at least. Part of their brief was to report back on the business they protected, especially if they had any suspicions about illegal activity, along with the type of work the company carried out. This was mainly for Titanium Securities protection, but also for opportunity, should Jacko and Tommy see any.
The rifle and pistol club, at Catterick Barracks was great for recruitment and gossip. Jacko and Tommy were recognised as go to guys, for people about to leave the force.
They also offered no interest, short term loans to squaddies. These loans were over no longer than 3 months and were, nearly almost, paid back before the term was up. Should anyone default Jacko would whisper in an ear or two, of guys still serving, and the loan would then be very quickly paid. One guy who took a loan, introduced them to a friend of his, Bobby Warren. Bobby was a big time crook out of Birmingham, who used the firearm facility when staying in his holiday cottage, in Ripon. He was a hunter, and when he could,

he went up to Scotland to shoot deer. He was a member of two different pheasant shoots, really enjoying anything to do with firearms. Most of his money was made from moving on stolen goods and he had contacts all over the country.

Over dinner at the Scotch Corner Hotel, on the junction of the A1 and A66, Tommy, Jacko and Bobby slowly warmed to each other and began to open up to each other. There was a lot of implied conversation but the meaning was clear enough to the three of them. Bobby was interested in using some of Tommy's storage facilities, he had dotted around Hartlepool, for some of his goods and also interested in buying anything Tommy should lay his hands on. Tommy insisted that there should always be a paper trail, that would show that goods stored by Tommy were there in good faith. Once the goods had been moved, the paper trail would be destroyed and the services paid for in cash.

"Where the hell can I get false documents from?" said Bobby.

"Me of course," replied Tommy. "I know someone who can provide documents, that will show I stored the goods in good faith, it's just an added cost that's all."

"How much is that going to cost?" asked Bobby.

"No more than 5% of the storage costs, and I can also get you similar documents for other warehouses, if you need them."

"Ok, well we will see the quality and then decide."

The evening wore on, with more than a bottle of brandy being consumed, before they all hit the sack in the early hours of the morning.

Bobby made a brief appearance at breakfast.

"Sorry boys, I have to move" he said, "I will be in touch next week and we can arrange something."

After handshakes all round Bobby left.

"Now" said Jacko, "who the hell do you know that can arrange false documents?"

"You!" came the reply.

"By fuck, you are knackered then. I can get you guns, ammo, clothing, even fucking hand grenades at a push, but what the fuck do I know about transport paper work?"

"Calm down, for fuck sake. I will get you some samples. You will work with Terry to provide forgeries, based on what I get you."

"Terry?"

"Yeah Terry. You and him have a great relationship. If he doesn't know we are a little wonky, he will do soon. So, you need to begin schooling him, on our shadier side of the business. Oh, and not a word to his mum."

"Ah right. Here we fucking go, now the penny drops. If Julie finds out what I'm doing, you are squeaky clean and still get to stoke the fire, whereas I get fucking salt in me coffee every morning."

Tommy couldn't help but laugh.

"Yeah, something like that. Now come on, we need to get back home and exercise some of last night out of us."

Tommy was right, Jacko and Terry had a great relationship, which was mainly based around Terry taking the piss out of Jacko, every time something technical came up and Jacko taking the piss about Terry's physique, which was beanpole thin not a muscle hiding anywhere.

Jacko sat Terry down the next week in the board room. Tommy good to his word had provided import documents from Germany, France and Japan.

"Now then Terry, what I tell you from now on, stays between us, you understand and I'm serious about this."

Terry's normally cocky demeanour change to serious.

"Sure, what's wrong?"

"Do you know what these are?" asked Jacko, pushing the documents across the table to Terry.

"Yeah of course, these are import documents, they sometimes get given to us with purchase documents for the computer shop."

"Good, so now you know what they are, it should be easy enough for you to forge them son."

"Of course these are simple enough, but why?"

"Because, not all of our business is above board and Tommy and me have never so much as been arrested because we are careful. Really careful. We will be holding some goods for a man that has borrowed them, from their rightful owner. Should the Police come sniffing, we want to be able to show we held them in good faith."

"I knew it!" grinned Terry. I fucking knew you two were dodgy. But yeah" he said more seriously, "I can knock these out all day long, once I build the templates."

"Make them good son, because if the man likes them, it may be a nice little side line that pays cash. You could use a little extra, couldn't you?"

"Fucking right I could. How much?"

"That's for another day, now listen up. Tommy has decided to trust you with this. There are only three people in the world now who know what we do. Half an hour ago, there were only two, so if I hear one tongue wagging, you are done with us. You understand?"

"Of course I do, and you know me better than that. I have never let you down and I never will."

"I know that Terry," said Jacko, laying a heavy hand on Terry's shoulder, "but it has to be said."

Terry, of course, was good to his word. The documents he provided were good enough to fool anyone, who didn't take the time to follow up fax and phone numbers.

He produced them in German, French, Italian and Japanese although in his own words.
"Fuck knows what all the Japanese says. I lifted most of it from Chinese takeaway menus!"

40

Tommy's relationship with Julie grew from strength to strength. He knew in his heart that she was everything he needed. He had stopped his Friday and Saturday nights out. They either ate at a restaurant or had nights in, with a take away. Comfortable with their own company, sometimes curled up together on the sofa watching whatever was on TV, happy to be together.
In January 1988, Tommy called for Julie as usual, on a Friday evening. They now spent every weekend together, but were not yet living together. Julie wanted to take it slower than Tommy and what Julie wanted, she got.
Tommy was more keen than ever to see her, as she had been away from work for a couple of days with "women's troubles."
As soon as Julie opened the door to Tommy, he knew something was wrong. She was dressed in an old jumper and jeans. No makeup on, her hair was a mess and her eyes all puffy from crying.
"What's wrong love?" Tommy's heart missed a beat.
"Come on in" she replied, "and sit down on the sofa."
Once Tommy was seated, she sat next to him and held his hands.
"Oh Tommy," she managed to say, before breaking down and sobbing. Great grief wracked sobs, each one hurting Tommy like a knife in his side. All he could do was wrap his arms around her and wait for her to stop crying. His big strong hands holding her, so gently.
"It's ok sweetheart" he whispered, "just let it all out," and she did. She cried like a child, cried until she was exhausted.

Eventually, she sat up and pulled away from him. Holding his hands in hers, she looked at him through red rimmed eyes.

"I've got the cancer Tommy. There's nothing to be done. I am dying and it's not long coming."

"What? No, you can't be," now it was Tommy's time to cry, tears running down his cheeks. "There must be something we can do. I have money sweetheart, more than you can ever imagine. We will get the best doctors."

"Tommy, its in my breasts, my liver and my bones. There's nothing to be done."

They spent the rest of the night holding each other, sometimes crying, sometimes dozing with the exhaustion of the emotion they both felt. Eventually, in the early hours of the morning, they went to bed. Wrapping themselves around each other they managed to sleep for a short while.

Tommy woke first. He got up and placed a call to Shafaq Hussain. He briefly explained the situation and asked him if he could help. Shaf promised to get back to him later that day.

When Julie got up, they ate a light breakfast and spoke. Tommy told Julie about the call he had made. She smiled and squeezed his hand.

"I will do anything you want, sweetheart, but don't get your hopes up." She then spoke about Terry. "I haven't told Terry yet. Can we do it together, today?"

"Of course we can sweetheart. He will be in the shop this morning. I will go collect him at 12."

"I need you to promise me, to look after him Tommy. Deep down, he's still a kid. I know he has loads of front but this will hurt him."

"Don't you worry about a thing Julie. Whatever happens, I will make sure he is alright, for as long as I draw breath.

For his age, he is already a wealthy young man, with a bright future ahead of him. I will make sure he will become the man you dreamed he would be. A man you can be proud of."

The afternoon was difficult for all three of them. Tommy now resigned to the worst, but still holding onto the hope that Shaf may find some miracle worker. Terry raged, he screamed and shouted. He threw a cup against the wall and started punching the wall, until Tommy restrained him, whispering in his ear,

"You got to be strong son, your mum needs you to be." Eventually he sagged, as if all the strength had left his body. The rest of the day, the three of them sat around Julie's small living room, drinking tea, chatting and watching TV.

Shaf called Tommy in the early evening, Julie had an appointment on Monday, with a consultant at a private hospital at Sheffield.

For the first time since they had been together, Tommy slept with Julie whilst Terry was in the house.

On Sunday, a semblance of normality returned to the house, buoyed by a false cheerfulness, that the specialist may be able to help. That afternoon, Tommy drove Julie to Sheffield. They stopped in a quiet hotel at Thorpe Hesley, before attending the private hospital on the outskirts of Sheffield, the following morning.

The Specialist, Doctor Nasser Ali, explained about the tests that would be carried out over the coming thirty six hours and at the end of that, he would be able to tell them exactly what was wrong. He finished the initial consultation with a warning.

"If what you have been told by your NHS surgeon is correct, then it is likely there is little, if anything, that can be done. However, we will explore every opportunity."

The hospital was the best money could afford. They were given a suite to stay in. Tommy sat around in their living room as Julie was, periodically, taken away for blood tests and scans.
On Wednesday morning, they sat down with Dr Ali. He explained each test that Julie had undertaken, what they were for and what they showed.
"It is, unfortunately, just as you have previously been told. You have a very aggressive form of cancer. Currently, there are no options for a cure. We may be able to prolong your life, with some drugs that are not available on the NHS."
"No" cut in Julie. "I don't want to sit around waiting to die, being kept alive longer than I should. Thank you, Doctor Ali, but I want to go home now."
Tommy asked Julie if she were sure, when they drove home.
Through pursed lips, she replied. "Yes." A quiet determination shrouded Julie. If she was going to die, she would die on her own terms.
Back in the office, Tommy briefed Jacko what was going on. Terry was also back, doing his best to be as upbeat and cocky as he normally was, and failing tremendously. There was a sadness to Terry, that radiated from him. People noticed, some asked him what was wrong but he just brushed off their concerns with having a bad day. Other than him, mum and Tommy, the only other person he opened up to, was Jacko. He told him everything, how he felt, how he wished he had been a better child, spent more time with his mum. Everything every nineteen year old would go through, when their mum was dying.
Julie refused chemotherapy saying, if she was going to die, she wanted to die when her time was due, not when the poisons used to slow down the spread of the cancer,

For his age, he is already a wealthy young man, with a bright future ahead of him. I will make sure he will become the man you dreamed he would be. A man you can be proud of."

The afternoon was difficult for all three of them. Tommy now resigned to the worst, but still holding onto the hope that Shaf may find some miracle worker. Terry raged, he screamed and shouted. He threw a cup against the wall and started punching the wall, until Tommy restrained him, whispering in his ear,

"You got to be strong son, your mum needs you to be."

Eventually he sagged, as if all the strength had left his body. The rest of the day, the three of them sat around Julie's small living room, drinking tea, chatting and watching TV.

Shaf called Tommy in the early evening, Julie had an appointment on Monday, with a consultant at a private hospital at Sheffield.

For the first time since they had been together, Tommy slept with Julie whilst Terry was in the house.

On Sunday, a semblance of normality returned to the house, buoyed by a false cheerfulness, that the specialist may be able to help. That afternoon, Tommy drove Julie to Sheffield. They stopped in a quiet hotel at Thorpe Hesley, before attending the private hospital on the outskirts of Sheffield, the following morning.

The Specialist, Doctor Nasser Ali, explained about the tests that would be carried out over the coming thirty six hours and at the end of that, he would be able to tell them exactly what was wrong. He finished the initial consultation with a warning.

"If what you have been told by your NHS surgeon is correct, then it is likely there is little, if anything, that can be done. However, we will explore every opportunity."

The hospital was the best money could afford. They were given a suite to stay in. Tommy sat around in their living room as Julie was, periodically, taken away for blood tests and scans.
On Wednesday morning, they sat down with Dr Ali. He explained each test that Julie had undertaken, what they were for and what they showed.
"It is, unfortunately, just as you have previously been told. You have a very aggressive form of cancer. Currently, there are no options for a cure. We may be able to prolong your life, with some drugs that are not available on the NHS."
"No" cut in Julie. "I don't want to sit around waiting to die, being kept alive longer than I should. Thank you, Doctor Ali, but I want to go home now."
Tommy asked Julie if she were sure, when they drove home.
Through pursed lips, she replied. "Yes." A quiet determination shrouded Julie. If she was going to die, she would die on her own terms.
Back in the office, Tommy briefed Jacko what was going on. Terry was also back, doing his best to be as upbeat and cocky as he normally was, and failing tremendously. There was a sadness to Terry, that radiated from him. People noticed, some asked him what was wrong but he just brushed off their concerns with having a bad day. Other than him, mum and Tommy, the only other person he opened up to, was Jacko. He told him everything, how he felt, how he wished he had been a better child, spent more time with his mum. Everything every nineteen year old would go through, when their mum was dying.
Julie refused chemotherapy saying, if she was going to die, she wanted to die when her time was due, not when the poisons used to slow down the spread of the cancer,

eventually failed. She wanted a head of hair when she was cremated.

Eventually, in March, she was moved into a hospice for palliative care. Drugs fed to her intravenously, kept the worst of the pain at bay, but she still suffered. On a cold, damp, overcast morning with Tommy holding one hand and Terry the other, she quietly passed away at just 38 years old.

As it was always done, back in the day, Julies death was announced on the Birth's, Deaths and Marriages page of the Hartlepool Mail. The notice finished with the cremation details, inviting family and close friends only. Tommy was concerned that people would turn up because of his relationship with Julie, rather than because of her. As it happened, the congregation for the service was small. The hearse left Strathmore House, followed by just one limousine, containing Terry and Tommy, Jacko was already at the crematorium, looking for anyone who might be trying to gain favour with Tommy, rather than to see Julie off but he had no need. Julie's dad had passed away eight years ago, her Mother passing when she was a child, she had no brothers or sisters. In all, there were just over twenty mourners, who were invited back to Strathmore House for sandwiches, tea and cake, after the service. The mood was sombre. Terry did well, speaking to everyone who attended, before sitting back down with Jacko, as Tommy did the rounds. It took less than 2 hours from the hearse leaving Strathmore House, to the last of the mourners saying goodbye to Tommy and Terry.

They had a short walk to the Old Durham's Working Men's Club, where they sat around a table in a smoky bar. The constant noise of traffic having a therapeutic, calming effect. After a round of brandies, Terry went onto Alpine lager whilst Tommy and Jacko both stuck

with Strongarm bitter. The conversation was muted, things said that were always said, lovely service, good turnout. No one really wanting to talk. It was Jacko that changed things up a little. "Right son" he said, looking at Terry, "we need to do something about your bones."
"My bones?" said Terry puzzled.
"Yeah, yer fucking bones. We need to get some meat on them boy. Your shoulders are as wide as your fucking hips, your pencil fucking thin. Every time we do a site visit, I'm worried you're going to blow away, if it's windy. So, starting tomorrow, you and me are going to exercise. You're going to learn to run, to lift weights. I'm going to teach you there's more to nutrition, than fucking burger and chips, and I'm going to beef you up a little. Fuck sake, you will never pull, looking like a fucking spelk. Now to do that, I need you to be local to me. So tonight, we collect your stuff from your house, along with anything you want of your mum's and you move in with me, at Seaton Carew."
"I'm not leaving my house," said Terry. "Fuck that."
"Listen son," said Jacko putting his big arm around Terrys shoulders," I have always been straight with you, always treated you like a man, so trust me. If you stay in that house, you won't find your mum there. All you'll find is ghosts and shadows. Your mum lives here now," he said, pushing a finger into Terrys chest over his heart, "and in here" he said, tapping his head. "It's the same with that big soppy sod 'n' all," he said nodding towards Tommy. "Fuck, it's the same for all of us. So let her live with you, not in the past, in a house that will become your prison. It's a rented property. Sanderson's auction house will clear it, once you have taken anything you want. Let the house go son, trust me."
"Are you sure?" asked Terry.

"Of course I am son. I was just saying to Tommy the other day, that I need a challenge and by fuck, turning you into a man, will keep me fucking busy for years!"

41

The following morning, Jacko and Terry collected his belongings, his mum's jewellery and a few photographs from the house he had lived in as long as he could remember. Closing the door for the final time and starting a new chapter in his live.
Jacko was good to his word, a trip up town followed, where Terry was kitted out with a decent pair of running shoes and some t-shirts and shorts for the gym. They went for their first run on the same evening, Jacko pushing Terry just hard enough as they ran along Warrior Drive, onto the seafront and back to Seaton Carew. They did a lap of the cricket club grounds before running back to Jacko's home.
"Thirty three minutes, nineteen seconds. Write it down son, every other day we will run that. Twenty five minutes is our target."
The next day after work, Jacko took Terry to a gym over the headland. It was grimy, most of the equipment had been there years, there were no pictures on the wall, with fancy motivational quotes. No expensive exercise machines, with flashing lights. Just weights and machines that held weights. Jacko put Terry to work. After twenty minutes, and five different exercises, Jacko said,
"That's yer lot."
"Thank fuck for that, I'm knackered," replied Terry.
"Fuck, for a bright kid you are fucking dumb. That's all you have to do, but you need to do it three times, it's called reps. Work it fucking out."
A bit like the odd couple Jacko and Terry really hit it off. Surprisingly, Terry proved to be a good pupil. Not only improving nearly every session they had, but he started

to log every piece of exercise they did, he then followed this up by keeping a food diary.

"Fucks sake," said Jacko one day, "you even geek over the gym."

"Piss off old man" laughed Terry, "I reckon another 45% improvement and I will be kicking your aged arse."

Friday nights became booze and take away night at Jacko's. Quite often, he, Terry and Tommy would have a couple of pints along the front, before going back to Jacko's for more booze and a curry. Over the months, the hurt that they all felt about Julie's loss began to soften and she often became the conversation piece, as they tucked into their curry.

Life was, slowly, getting back to normal. The businesses continued to thrive. The security arm especially was thriving. Placing security guards was a significant part of the business. There were still some large manufacturers in the town and the surrounding areas. The rates that Jacko offered, the lure of using ex-squaddies and the reputation that Tommy had for being a stand up business man, made Titanium Security the go to supplier for trustworthy security.

Tommy secured two further warehouses, along with the small space he had at Titanium headquarters, one at Middlesbrough just off the A19, the other not far from Catterick just off the A1. Both were almost exclusively manned with ex-squaddies, that Jacko vetted and recommended. Each warehouse had a manager in place, that had served in logistics in the Army. They ran like clockwork and were, for the most part, legitimate businesses. Jacko was given the honour of naming this new arm of Tommy's business. He chose, Armysecure. Tommy recruited a marketing firm who produced great mail shot fliers, focusing on the links Tommy's businesses had with ex-service men.

The warehouses were soon close to capacity. Tommy identified an opportunity to distribute from the warehouses, and soon they had a fleet of transit vans and small 8 ton lorries, delivering stock all over the North for their clients. In total, they had over 100 ex-squaddies working for them. If they were highly regarded by their business partners, the serving squaddies saw them as almost God like figures and they were always made welcome at the firing range. Both were given lifelong memberships to the range, for services to the Army community.

Tommy was doing more and more storage for Bobby Warren. It was normally an artic lorry in, followed by a number of smaller wagons collecting the goods, over the following days.

The paperwork that Terry produced was exceptional, with fax and phone numbers to actual continental firms. The paperwork was sufficiently vague, yet official looking enough, to pass any visual inspection. Fortunately, Bobby's network was professional enough, to make sure that the paperwork was never inspected.

Bobby had a couple of warehouses himself, that mixed the legitimate arm of his business with the illicit side. He paid Tommy on time and in cash, normally at the Catterick base where they, along with Jacko, would shoot together.

Bobby did on occasion make use of Terry's skills, for stock in his own warehouse. He once asked Tommy, if Terry was an asset that he would ever consider releasing?

"I could use a man like that."

Tommy replied "I bet you fucking could. No and no again, at the risk of our relationship."

"Thought so," replied Bobby, "and understood."

42

In September 1988, Terry turned 20. He was still building his body up but he looked significantly different. His arms and legs had gained bulk, his shoulders and neck were bigger and his stomach, that was always flat, was now flat and hard. The day of his birthday, Tommy, Jacko and Terry took the day off work. They met at Jacko's for breakfast, a traditional British fry up, sausage, egg, bacon, baked beans, mushrooms and black pudding. The black pudding was served cold and un-fried, at Tommy's insistence.

"Spicier this way," he told Jacko and Terry, and after initial reservations, they both agreed Tommy was right. After breakfast, they took a short walk across the Warrior Park Estate, that was still a growing development of detached houses. Tommy led them to a 4 bedroomed house, in Ark Royal Close. The house was furnished expensively. The original builder supplied kitchen, had been ripped out and replaced with a bespoke hand built one finished with marble work surfaces. The en-suite to the master bedroom, along with the family bathroom, had also been extensively improved. The master bedroom featured built in wardrobes and a king sized bed with silken sheets.

Having toured the property, they sat on the leather suite in the living room, that looked out over a South facing garden. A gift wrapped box sat on a coffee table. Tommy chucked a bunch of keys at Terry.

"Happy birthday son," he said.

"What's this?" Terry replied.

"The keys to this house, it's yours. Well actually it's mine, but it's yours to use rent free for as long as you want it."

"Fuck sake Tommy. Thank you."

"Yeah well" added Jacko, "much as I like you, you were cramping my style, living in my place. I aint had a shag in ages."

"Now open your present." said Tommy. Terry did and inside was a bottle of washing up liquid, some bleach, dusters, glass cleaner and brillo pads.

"Everything you need to keep this place clean. There's a lawn mower and strimmer in the shed out back. By fuck, you look after this place. There's a business card in the bottom of the box, for a cleaning company that I use, to look after my gaff. I suggest you give them a call, they are expecting to hear from you."

"Of course I will and thank you again Tommy."

"Terry you earn good money now. Great money. You have a rent free house, a company car, the stocks I bought us in the Microsoft mob are going up quicker than a whore's knickers. You are already a wealthy young man.

On Monday we will meet and look to give you some financial responsibilities. I have an old mate Gary Tanners. He's marketing some real top end places, up at Wynyard. I will lend you a deposit for one. Gary will find you a tenant. The rent will more than pay your mortgage and the projected increase in value in the properties, make it a sure fire earner. Once you have this one under your belt, I suggest you buy another. Save some of what you earn every month son, you never know what's around the corner and, apart from the odd hiccup, houses will always make you money."

"Now all that bollocks is out of the way, tell us about Sally," said Jacko.

"What, not Sally out of accounts?" asked Tommy, innocently, although he, like everyone in the business, knew that the two were a couple.

"The very same," said Jacko. "Terry's dipping his wick. He has been for a couple of weeks."

Terry grinned, "What can I say? I'm a chick magnet."

"Is it serious?" asked Tommy.

"It will be on Saturday night. She has promised to do anything I want, for my birthday."

"Fucking hell!" said Jacko. "I was once tomming this girl, she was younger than me, a lot younger. She was really fit. Her old man was a bit vanilla in the sack, she wanted a bit of slap with her tickle, so I obliged. She told me one time after a shag, that she would do anything for me. I asked her anything do you promise? She said yes, so I told her blow jobs for life. I still see her occasionally, although she lives miles away now, but do you know what, she's good to her word and bloody good at sucking cock too! She was the only bird I ever thought I could live with, maybe I should have stuck with her but it is what it is."

"Fucking hell," said Tommy "listen to that twat! It's his fucking birthday and you want to pollute our ears, with your perversions, you sad bastard."

Jacko grinned, "yeah you're right, but like I said, she was good."

"Right," said Tommy. "Now the next part of your present." He reached behind the sofa and pulled out a pair of boxing gloves. "Now that Jacko has gotten you fit, I need to teach you how to fight, how to defend yourself, mark you. I'm not doing this so you can become a bully. Mondays and Wednesdays we will go to Feeny's gym and I will teach you how to box. That will involve exercise, skipping, bag work and eventually, when you're ready, sparring. You have a lot going for you, a career, a good car, a house. Some people your age will resent that, you need to be able to defend yourself."

"Cool. When will I be good enough to have a match?"

"That's not part of the plan, but if you stick to it, maybe a year, 18 months."

"Right" said Tommy, standing up. "Come on, we are going for a walk." They left the new estate and walked up Queens Street, which is part of old Seaton Carew. A ribbon of the North Sea appearing, as they crested a slight bank, where Queens Street crossed Lawson Road. Slowly, the sea opened out. Marine Drive that ran along the seafront became visible, as did the promenade on the other side of Marine Drive.

"I never get tired of this view" said Jacko "I always feel at home and at peace when I see the sea and the beach."

"Yeah, I know what you mean," said Tommy. "There's something hypnotic about the coast. Something that makes life seem easier, better."

"Right, come on," said Tommy. They stayed on the village side of the seafront and walked past the Staincliffe Hotel.

The Hotel was once a private house and from the frontage, it has fantastic views over the bay, that ran from the Headland of Hartlepool to the North Gare, or as it is known locally the slag wall, which is on the North side of the mouth of the river Tees, a small concrete pier that is good for fishing, whilst protecting the North side of Tees mouth from sea erosion. The South end of the Staincliffe had a Chapel built on it. This was now the Chapel Bar and was popular with Jacko and Terry, when they fancied a beer. It had a decent pool table and a good juke box, mixing up chart toppers with historic hits. Just past the Hotel was a row of twelve, four storey terraced houses. They were big and opulent, built in the 19th Century. Tommy led them in to the courtyard that fronted the properties and up the steps, to the looming front door of one of the middle houses.

"I bought this place last year and have had people in since then, doing it up. You're my first guests. Come on in."

"Fuck sake! You kept this quiet" said Jacko.

"Yeah well, everyone has their secrets," said Tommy. "Let's start in the cellar." They walked down a flight of stairs off the wide entrance hall. "I had to have this tanked out because of the damp. I reckon the high tides made this place wet." The cellar had plaster free walls, that were whitewashed. Spot lights made the space, that had no natural light, bright and comforting. The space was filled with weight lifting equipment. "My own personal gym."

"Very nice" said Jacko, casting an appreciative eye over the equipment. "How the other half live!"

"Right, come on," said Tommy, "ground floor now."

To the front, a large living room with a grand fireplace. The views out of the ten foot high windows were restricted by the wall to the front of the courtyard, but the dirty grey North Sea was still easy to see. To the back of the ground floor, was a huge kitchen diner that looked out onto a big walled back garden. The kitchen was black, black units and black marble work surfaces.

On the first floor, was another living room, this time with uninterrupted views of the sea, the headland to the North and Redcar and beyond to the South.

"Fuck sake. This is some place," said Jacko "and look at those views."

A small bathroom, a large kitchen diner and a large master bedroom, with ensuite, completed the first floor. The next 2 floors contained 2 more bedrooms and a bathroom each. The finish to the house was immaculate. It was clear that no money had been spared, and no corners cut, to provide a house of elegance and

opulence. The three of them sat in the first floor living room window, facing the sea. All of them drank tea.
"This is why I bought this place and every time I have visited the house over the last 7 months, this view has always been the same and always different. The bay will never change, not in my lifetime at least, but the tides and the weather do. I have seen water smashing over the promenade outside of the Staincliffe and the sea so calm, it looked like it was a field of bluey green rather than water. At the risk of sounding poetic, it's breath taking."
"You poetic? No fucking chance of that," said Jacko, as diplomatic as he ever was, "but I have to grant you I will be visiting you more often here, than I ever did in your old gaff."
"Me too," said Terry. "The view is super. I wish me mum could have seen it."
"So do I" said Tommy, his voice barely more than a whisper.
They sat in silence for a few minutes, just taking in the view. Each of them lost in their own thoughts. It was left to Jacko to break the quiet.
"Fucking hell. We are sat here like 3 old men. It's the boy's birthday for fucks sake. It's ten past eleven. Why aint we in a fucking pub?"
"Yeah you're right," said Tommy. "How about a game of snooker around the club, then we will do a tour of the village."
The afternoon was filled with laughing and piss taking. Jacko doing most of the piss taking but for some reason seeming to be the butt of most of the jokes. Jacko and Tommy reminisced, about when they first met. Terry loved to hear them talking about the old days.
Jacko took credit for teaching Tommy everything he knows about guns and shooting,

"He couldn't hit a barn door with gravel from 3 feet, until I schooled him. He fucking well owes me everything."
"Fucking owe you everything, you ginger minger! I have paid you back a dozen times over, since I offered you a job. I have carried you and wiped your arse ever since. Even birthday boy here has had to put you in his haversack and carry you into the 20th century."
So, it went on, as did the day. For the most of it, Terry was happy to be in the company of the two guys he admired most, in all of the world. Their banter never stopped and the more they slagged each other off, the more it was apparent that they loved each other.
Sometime in the afternoon, Terry said to them both,
"I hope I have a friend like you two one day."
Jacko answered, "You do son. You have both of us. All you need to do, is to get a few miles under your belt with us. You are family to us. An apprentice maybe or the inbred cousin, something like that, but family nevertheless."
"Maybe he's adopted?" chipped in Tommy. "A charitable act, by two gentlemen."
"Adopted my arse! You two cunts, wouldn't be able to open the fucking box of a computer, never mind set one up and use one. It's me looking after the stone age Neanderthals, more like. You two are my charity cases. A couple of dinosaurs, that need a young handsome twenty year old executive to keep them tech savvy and up to date. You would be fucking extinct without me."
"Are you finished?" asked Jacko.
"Yeah why?" Terry said, turning to face him.
"Fucking good job" said Tommy, cuffing Terry around the back of the head. "Now go get a fucking round in."
The afternoon dragged on into the evening. The Marine, The Seaton Hotel, The Cricket Club and even the Golf Club being visited before they wander staggered into the

Chapel bar for a last drink. They then headed back to Jacko's for a Chinese take away, that no one really needed or wanted, but as was the way since time began, it would be consumed regardless, with the ceremony of 'left over' breakfast the next day.

It was Monday morning before Tommy and Jacko saw Terry again. He walked into the business canteen whistling and with a swagger in his step.

"Here's the cat that got the cream over the weekend," said Tommy.

"Yeah, you might say that," replied Terry. "Lots of fucking cream."

"Come on then, pull up a chair, tell us all about it" chipped in Jacko.

"Jacko! Piss off you old pervert. Don't you say a word, Terry. Enjoy the moment, don't pollute it by telling him what happened."

43

Over the following 2 years, the business continued to flourish. Tommy added another warehouse to his portfolio, just outside of Newcastle. As with the others, it was almost totally staffed with ex-squaddies. A fleet of small lorries and vans were added and it was soon bringing in great revenue. Bobby Warren continued to use Tommy's facilities but less often. "I'm thinking of turning straight," he confided in Tommy one night. "I have enough money now. The businesses I have are doing well and plod seems to be getting their act together. I'm too old to do time."
"Yeah, I know where you are coming from," said Tommy. "It's just the thrill of it. I love thinking I got one over on the establishment. It's a rush."
In 1989, Tommy's mother, Nancy, died suddenly of a heart attack. Tommy always remembered her as a stout lady, fat but strong with it, but over the last 10 years or so, she had gained a lot of weight. Tommy had continued to put money on the table every Friday. He made a point of dropping in sometime during the day, with a bunch of flowers and a little cash. More than was needed, for sure, but what wasn't spent on the house and bills, was spent by Tommy's dad at the Quoit Club. At the end of 1989, Tommy senior died. He had been a smoker since he was 10 years old. Tommy could hardly remember seeing him without an untipped Woodbine or Capstan full strength in his mouth. The 2 fingers that held a cigarette of his smoking hand, were a browny yellow colour. When death came to visit Tommy senior, it was quick. Just 2 weeks after being diagnosed with cancer, he was dead.

After the funeral and wake, Tommy returned to his seafront house and sat at dusk, watching the lights on the ships crossing the bay come on.
'Just me all on my todd now,' he thought to himself. 'No more family to visit.'

44

In February 1990, Tommy took a phone call from one of his police contacts, Jeff Wainwright. Jeff was an Inspector at Hartlepool and went on to explain that they had received intelligence from Merseyside police, that Tommy was storing stolen goods. The Yorkshire and Durham constabularies were working together, to get search warrants for the Teesside and Catterick warehouses. These would be issued sometime tomorrow morning and the premises were scheduled to be searched later that day.
"I can't do anything to stop this happening" Jeff told Tommy "I just wanted you to know in advance."
"I appreciate the call. Of course, there is nothing in the allegations but thank you anyway. I will see you at the next fund raiser" said Tommy, before hanging up.
Immediately he was off the phone to the copper, Tommy phoned Bobby Warren. In total, Bobby had 36 pallets of hooky goods, shared between the two warehouses.
"Who the fuck has talked?" asked Bobby.
"I have a good idea," replied Tommy "but firsts things first. Can you collect today or would you rather us move them for you?"
"No worries buddy. I will have lorries at both sites before 6 pm. They will be long gone, before plod gets up tomorrow morning."
"Great stuff. I will see you Saturday at the range and we will have a chat about who and what we should do about it."
Next, Tommy was on the phone to Jacko. He explained the situation and asked Jacko to go to the Catterick site to oversee the collection, whilst he would go to the Teesside one. Tommy then phoned Terry and told him he would pick him up in twenty minutes.

On the road to the Teesside warehouse, Tommy explained to Terry what was going on. He wanted Terry to double check the site computers, for any signs of his dealings with Bobby Warren and delete any incriminating evidence.

"There should be none," he went on to explain "as our dealings are pretty much word of mouth and the paper trails you produce. Once we have finished with Teesside, we will shoot over to Catterick to do the same and then back to Hartlepool and go about our business as normal tomorrow."

Everything went to plan with Bobby's lorries on site, loaded and despatched before the 6pm that they were due. The areas that had held Bobby's knock off stock, were cleaned and then backfilled with existing stock, making the areas looked used, not recently emptied. Everything looked perfectly normal.

The next day, Tommy and Jacko were working from the head office, when calls came through at 2:30 pm. Both warehouses were subject to search warrants. Once they had been made aware, Tommy headed off with Terry to Catterick, whilst Jacko covered Teesside. The search teams found nothing at all, other than stored goods for reputable businesses across the country.

"Tell me again," said Tommy, to the Inspector responsible for the search at Catterick. "Who said we were storing stolen goods?"

"We had a tipoff, is all," came the terse reply.

"Well I hope your next one, is better than the one you have had regarding my storage facilities. I have had not so much as a speeding ticket and you want to risk my reputation, based on a tip off? Are you fucking mad?"

"Mr Flounders, I can assure you the information has come from a reliable source."

"Well it fucking aint reliable, when it comes to my warehouses, is it? Now if you have finished, we are coming to the busiest time of the day. Also, please jot down your name and badge number on that sheet of paper, and make sure a copy of the search warrant is left with reception.

I have been a supporter of police charities for over 15 years now. Had you made enough enquiries, you would have been aware of my reputation. I have to tell you, officer, I value my reputation above everything. Should I or my businesses get any bad feedback in the press, or be subject to gossip, I will instruct my solicitors to take this further. So please make sure, whichever of your squad leak details to the press, for a bung, that they keep their fucking mouths shut!"

"I can assure you, Mr Flounders, that none of my men would ever do such a thing."

"You can assure me of nothing, Inspector. To be honest, this whole episode has tarnished my view of the Police force. Now, if you have nothing else you need, please get you and your men off my property here and Teesside."

It took less than 3 hours, from Tommy receiving the call, to both sites being cleared of police.

"Fucking hell Tommy," said Terry. "You kicked arse."

"It might have been different, if I never got the tip off son. Remember the old saying, keep your friends close and your enemies closer. A certain copper in Hartlepool, has just earned a nice little bung.

On Saturday, me 'n' Jacko will go up the shooting club, to let off steam and discuss this. Do you want to come?"

"Fucking right I do," came the reply.

45

Terry had to be signed in, as a guest, and was not allowed to handle any of the guns or ammunition. He was, however, allowed to observe and was shocked by the noise and the lethality of the weapons being discharged. The three of them had a meal in the bar afterwards.

"I can't get over how quickly it actually happens. There is literally no time, from the second you pulled the trigger, to the hole appearing in the target."

"What you have to understand Terry, the very single principle of every piece of munition, is that it is a killing machine. Its sole function is to do enough damage to a human body, to kill it. Most bullets are designed to break down on impact. The result, if you like, is one bullet hits you but ten or fifteen fragments leave you. They spread and shred, everything they come into contact with, bone, tissue, blood vessels, everything. A shoulder hit from a rifle, would be lethal, in most cases.

I know those fucking vid games, you are always playing, glorify killing but it's hard son. Hearing a man scream after you have shot him. Walking past a body knowing that seconds ago, he was a son, a husband, a father and now he's just detritus, waiting for a body bag, a statistic and a grave marker. There aint no glory in war son," said Jacko, his eyes a million miles away in memories he wished he didn't have.

"And on that cheerful note, shall we order dessert, before you say enough to put a damper on the rest of the weekend?" chipped in Tommy.

"Yeah, you're right Tommy. Sorry Terry but I had to let you know the reality. If you want in as a member, we can sort that but I just wanted you to know, what you would be handling."

An hour or so later, the three of them took a table away from the bar. The regulars knew enough, to know not to disturb them and that when they were ready to socialise, they would be at the bar buying beers.
"So," said Tommy, "a while ago Jacko and myself had a little deal going with a man called Alby from Liverpool. For a while it was sweet but it turned sour. We left on bad terms. I'm guessing it is this guy, who fingered us for the storing of stolen goods. I'm not sure he's the kind of man who would offer this up voluntary, but if he was in a corner, I have no doubt he would try to save his own skin. Offering us up, would buy him time before he had to finger bigger fish at home, if he hasn't already. Jacko is going across to Liverpool, next week, to sus out what he can. Would you like to go with him?"
"Sure" said Terry "I would love to."
"Understand now," said Tommy, "this isn't a game. This is the real thing, the risks are minimum or I would not let you go, but they are still real. You do whatever Jacko tells you, whenever he tells you, no fucking questions, you just do it ok?"
"Absolutely."
"You will be leaving around 3pm on Monday. This will give you time to make sure everyone at the shop, and head office, knows you will be gone and what you expect of them whilst you are away."
The rest of the day, after a quick meeting with Bobby Warren, was spent catching up with old friends and talking to the two sergeants, that looked after the money that they had set aside, to help servicemen with a short-term need. Tommy and Jacko had been talking for a while, about the pressures that ex-service men had, when they left the Army. Many actually ended up on the streets, simply because they had no clue how to get a

property, once they were back in civvies. Once they left the Army, the Army washed their hands of them.

Tommy said, "perhaps we should purchase a couple of flats, through the business, and put leavers in for a short term, whilst we support them finding their feet in civvy street."

The general consensus was, it may be a good thing.

"I will contact Gary Tanners after the weekend and get him to check out what properties are available, that would be suitable."

Monday came, Jacko and Terry headed off to Liverpool. Tommy caught up with Gary Tanners and explained what they were looking for. He told Gary that they needed two and or three bedroom properties, along with 1 bed flats in and around Catterick, Middlesbrough and Hartlepool. He then met with his accountants, to discuss what would be the best way to fund this. It turned out that Tommy could set up a charity and that once approved, it would allow him to do what he wanted, tax free. He would be able to take donations, from likeminded business partners and individuals, which would be written off against tax. In reality not costing them anything. Plans were put in place, for "New Drill" to be registered as a charity, for ex-service men who had either fallen off the grid or needed help when first leaving the services, with their families.

46

On Tuesday, Jacko and Terry set about finding Alby.
"We will start at his warehouse," said Jacko. "The flash bastard always attracted attention by driving top of the range Jags. One drive past the car park and we will know if he is in."
Sure enough, a bright red Jaguar sat in a prime parking spot, in the car park.
"Looks like he's home," said Jacko.
"What now?" asked Terry
"Now the boring bit. We sit and wait."
Terry reached onto the back seat, for a bottle of coke and a sandwich.
 "Lunch time then," he said.
"Go steady with the coke son. We can't pop over the road for a piss, so if you do need to, it's going to be back into the bottle. The less you drink the better."
Just before lunch, Alby headed out. Jacko was about to follow but waited as a second car, with 2 guys in it, trailed Alby from the car park.
"That's interesting, a ford Sierra with two guys in it. That screams coppers all day long," said Jacko.
"What do we do now then?" asked Terry.
"Follow them, if we can. Hopefully, those two in the Sierra are more interested in what's going on in front of them, than behind them."
Alby visited three different, run down houses in Toxteth.
"Those have to be whorehouses," said Jacko. "They even have red fucking lights in the windows."
After visiting the last house, Alby drove out of the city, still being followed, until he reached a large detached house in the small village of Appleton. He parked on the drive, then walked over to the guys in the Sierra, had a quick chat with them and they drove off, leaving Alby to

enter the house. Jacko was able to follow the Sierra, back into Liverpool. Twenty minutes after leaving Alby's house, the Sierra pulled into a Police Station yard and the 2 men disappeared into the building.

"Got ya," whispered Jacko.

"Right son, let's go find a camera shop. We need to get some pictures of Alby with the two coppers. After that, we can head off home and decide what to do next, with Tommy."

Jacko bought a Nikon SLR, with a telephoto lens.

"This is a better lens," said Terry "why not get this one?"

"It's twice the size son. Don't forget, we are going to be sat in a car taking pictures. It's too unwieldly. You need to be able to lift, focus and take a picture, in as short a time as possible. Remember, we are supposed to be undercover. If the coppers or Alby rumble us, it will bring a lot of heat onto us."

The next two days, Jacko and Terry shadowed Alby and the police men, that were following him. Wednesday followed a similar pattern, with Jacko and Terry arriving at Alby's around 06:30. The police arrived some forty minutes later, with Alby leaving 15 minutes after that. He started at the warehouse and then moving on to a pub, a brothel and a private flat, where he spent 2 hours, before heading off home. He then wandered over to say goodbye to the coppers, before heading in. All of his actions were captured on camera, with the addresses of each premises he visited being recorded.

Thursday proved to be more interesting. Alby visited a few properties as before, but then followed the coppers back to the police station and went inside for the best part of two hours.

"I guess that settles it then. He has turned. He gets to do what he has always done, by selling out everyone and everything he knows, the twat." The anger clear on Jacko's voice.

On Friday, they spent the morning in Liverpool's main library, working backwards through the local papers. Over the last seven weeks, the police had made three high profile arrests, including an Irish gang that was caught with a lockup full of drugs. Photocopies of the relevant articles made, Jacko and Terry headed back home, on Friday lunch time.

Friday night, the three of them met at Titanium Security's head office. Jacko briefing Tommy on exactly what had transpired, during the time they had spent in Liverpool.

"So that's it then. He has sold out. No wonder people are being turned over by the coppers," said Tommy. "Now we know, what do we do? We can't let this go. The coppers probably know we have supplied Alby with knock off gear in the past. They won't be able to do nowt about that now, as to bring us in, would mean doing him as well. Now we are aware they are looking at us, we will need to keep clean for a while, but what do we do about Alby?"

"We should do what we promised him before. Go to the papers with what we have. Them Scousers are queer fuckers. They hate everyone else in the country but hate coppers and grasses more. Give a journalist what we have, pictures, dates, times. Coppers following a face about, protecting him as he grasses others up! The press will have a field day. Alby will be wanted by every criminal in Liverpool. He will be done there." said Jacko.

"Terry what do you think?" asked Tommy.

"What about his family, will they be targets too?"

"Probably not. If anyone topped his family they would lose popular support and have the whole of the Merseyside police looking for them. His family would

have to lie low but would be safe. Alby on the other hand, would not be safe anywhere, for the rest of his life"
"OK I say we publish," Terry said grinning.
"Right, let's get the roll of film into Boots tomorrow morning. We should have the pictures back by lunch time Tuesday. Wednesday, we go find us a journalist, who will go to print. Now, it's half past beer o'clock. You guys fancy a couple up the Chapel Bar?"
"Sounds good," said Jacko.
"Count me in" added Terry.

47

The weekend passed as most others did, a few beers with a curry Friday night, on Saturday the three of them went to Catterick. Tommy and Jacko shot for a while, followed by lunch in the bar. Tommy told Jacko and Terry what he had asked Garry Tanners to look out for and what his accountant had told him.

"This country does nowt for ex-squaddies, so we will have to look after them ourselves. I am sure we will be able to get plenty of our customers on board. We can do the basics, by giving leavers details on how to get property, to find a job etcetera, and look after those that can't handle it, until they can. We won't sort out everyone's problems but we will help, how and when we can."

Saturday evening, they returned to Hartlepool and went their separate ways, planning to meet again Tuesday afternoon, once Terry had collected the developed pictures.

On Tuesday, they met in the boardroom of Titanium Security.

"I've had a change of heart," said Tommy. "If we go to the press, we are signing his death warrant. I know he deserves it, but some of the people out there would give him a nasty end. What do you think about giving Alby a copy of everything we have and allowing him 24 hrs to get out of the country. I have been onto the travel agents this morning. There are two flights a day from Liverpool to Spain. We could put Andrew Leeson or Pudding Smithies on a plane, give them enough cash for a couple of days in Spain and they could track him there."

"Are you sure Tommy? He's turned, he is a grass. He may not be ready to give it all up. He might fuck off for a

while but we would never know if he came back into the country. He's a fucking grass mate, I say dob him in"
"I am sure Jacko."
"In that case then, yeah, it might work. I can't think of a better option."
"I know it has it's risk's but what can I do? I don't want to kill a man by someone else's hand. Can you remember, we were chatting with him, after the TV job we did with him. He said he moves a lot of cash offshore. He should be fine for cash for years. Can you organise a couple of shadow for Thursday's flights? I will arrange the tickets."
"No problem. Shall we meet back here in a couple of hours? One car or two?"
"Two. Terry, you can ride shotgun with Jacko. I will take my own car, I want to deliver this personally."
"Unnecessary risk Tommy. You know that."
"Yeah, I know, but what can I say. I need to do this."
On Wednesday morning, Tommy walked into the reception area of Alby's warehouse, just after 11am. Alby had been there for 2 hours. He gave the receptionist a Manilla envelope, marked for the attention of Alby Green, strictly private and urgent. Inside the envelope, was a copy of all the pictures Jacko and Terry had taken, along with a list of the premises Alby had visited. Most importantly the time and date, with corresponding photographs of Alby, walking into a police station flanked by two officers. Lastly, on a plain piece of paper was a telephone number, of a top up mobile phone, that Tommy had paid cash for the previous day. Less than 30 minutes later, the phone rang.
"Who is this?" said Alby, doing his best to sound menacing.
"This is the second time, I have had to threaten you with going to the papers Alby. Now after you have said

goodnight to plod today, take a walk down to that pub on the green where you live, I have some things to tell you."
"Fucking Tommy Flounders!"
"Yes, now make sure you are there alone. You know me well enough, to know I am careful. One sign of plod, or any of your guys, and I am gone and gone for good. No second chances. So turn up, and turn up alone."
"And if I don't?"
"Then I pay a visit to your local newspaper. You know how they like a gangster strapline, and you being in the old bills pocket, will suit them just fine. See you later Alby."
Tommy hung up and said to Jacko, "Do you and Terry want to take a walk around that village? It's surrounded by fields. There must be somewhere I can have eyes on the pub but out of sight, until Alby turns up and turns up alone"
"No problems buddy"
"Good stuff. Whilst you two are taking in all nature has to offer, I will go to the pub for a beer. Give it a look over, see the lie of the land. Should things go pear shaped, I need to know the best way out. Once you have had a good look around, come in and we will have some lunch."
A couple of hours, later the three of them sat in the garden of the pleasant pub, enjoying pie, veg, chips and gravy.
"How does the environment look Jacko? Any easy outs for me?"
"Should be pretty simple, to be honest. If anything goes wrong, you can jump into a car with Terry already at the wheel. I will block the exit after you leave, it's only five minutes to a motorway. If you sit in the garden, there are two exits. Just take the one nearest the kids play area, Terry will park up there."

"If the three of us sit up on the Church car park, we can see the pub and both ways up the road. It don't open again till 5.00. If anyone gets here early, they will stick out like a sore thumb. If anyone suspicious arrives after you and Alby sit down together, we will call you. Any call from us, don't waste time answering, just leg it."
"Right boys, we have a plan," replied Tommy. "Now tuck in, before it goes cold."
The afternoon was spent parked up, watching the pub. Both cars were used, with a rota of one watching, whilst two rested their eyes.
"Doesn't this get to you?" Terry asked Jacko.
"Not really. We have given the place a good check over. We have an out plan, if we need one, and to be honest the risks are minimal. We need to be alert but Tommy is no dummy. He will smell out any kind of setup. But stay alert. If you see something that doesn't feel right, shout up, ok buddy?"
"Sure."

48

Tommy arrived at the pub just after it opened. He bought a pint and settled himself in the walled garden, close to the car park and with his back to the wall. Twenty minutes later, Alby arrived G & T in hand and the customary snarl on his face.
"Right, what the fuck do you want?"
"I want to know, why the fuck you are grassing up everyone you have done business with, to the fucking cops, you cunt? Now before you decide to play the hard man with me, remember we have done this before. I still don't know if I leave here and go home, or leave here and go to the press. So stop being a twat and tell me what's going on."
Alby took a swig of his drink and sat quiet for a moment.
"Remember Pok face? He worked closely for me, was me right hand man to be honest?"
"Yeah go on"
"Well, he got caught with a kilo of cocaine and instead of doing some bird, he sold me out to the Bill. When they pulled me, he had told them just about everything. They could only hold me 24 hours but it would have taken weeks, to clear me warehouses of all of the dodgy stock. They had search warrants prepared for 2 warehouses, the knocking shops, the flat I keep a girl in, and my home. I had to roll over or I was done. I swear to you, I will kill Pok face once I find out where he is."
"So instead of Pok face doing some time, he sold you out?"
"Yeah"
"And instead of you doing some time, you sold every other fucker out?"
"It would have been 20 years. I aint doing that stretch and even if I did, there would have been people nervous

enough about what I knew, to have me shanked in jail. I would have been as good as dead."

Tommy though for a moment. "Yeah, I guess you would have been, but you fingered me, so it's now personal. I can't let this go Alby, you know that"

"So what are you going to do then, go to the press?"

"Nope I am going to give you these." Tommy handed over an envelope. "Inside are two airplane tickets to Spain, Alicante. One leaves tomorrow at 10 am, the other leaves tomorrow at 5 pm. Take your pick but be on one. I have eyes on both. If you don't go, then I go to the press. The first time we met, you told me you had cash abroad and a pad in Spain. Well it's time to put your feet up, for good."

"I can't do that. I have businesses. My family, for fucks sake."

"You have lawyers. I have no doubt, your warehouses are now free of anything crooked. Your lawyers will sell the businesses as going concerns. Move your whorehouses on, if you can. When you are ready, move your family across. Spain has no extradition treaty with the UK. I am offering you an out Alby, an out you should have taken as soon as the coppers came knocking. There is no alternative."

Alby swirled the ice around in his G & T. He looked up at Tommy.

"Why are you doing this? Why didn't you just go to the papers?"

"I aint a grass and I am sure if the locals got to you, before the coppers did, you would have a hard death. As much as a cunt you are, I don't want that on my hands."

Alby picked up the envelope, containing the tickets.

"I will be on the 5 o'clock plane."

"Good man"

Tommy stood, Alby held out his hand to shake Tommy's.

"Not a fucking chance of that. You're a grass, you cunt!" With that Tommy walked out of the pub, jumped into the car with Terry and they set off, on the long drive home. Two days later, Andrew Leeson made a call to Jacko, confirming that Alby was now living in his villa in Spain. Unfortunately for Alby, it wasn't only Tommy that suspected and then proved his collusion with the Police force. It had become common knowledge around the underworld of Liverpool. Some bent copper taking a bung and feeding his details, in exchange for the cash. Seven months after he left the city, he was found dead in his swimming pool, tortured, and shot.

49

Over the following 4 years, the businesses flourished. Titanium Security opened satellite offices, in Doncaster and Carlisle, staffing over 100 customer premises with 24/7 security.
Armysecure warehousing opened up two further sites, one just off the A1 at Sherburn in Elmet and one on the M62 at Leeds. Both sites offered storage, along with delivery and collection services, and wherever possible were manned with ex-service personnel, mainly Army, but also with a smattering of ex-RAF and Navy too.
Jacko and Tommy would make a point of visiting a site a month and would be introduced to each new employee. The camaraderie that Jacko built, with almost every employee, was phenomenal. He remembered so many personal details, it was unbelievable.
"You know these men so well, you put me to shame." Tommy once commented.
"Back in the day, the first time you met someone could be the last. I just felt it was important, to honour their memory and it became habit to remember something about everyone I met, now it's become important to me. I like to remember something about everyone."
Andrew Leeson and Pudding Smithies were both taking active, responsible roles in Armysecure; liaising with warehouse and transport managers; seeking out new recruits and generally trouble shooting as and when needed, whilst Tommy and Jacko were responsible for new and existing contracts.

Bobby Warren was now fully legitimate and taking a back seat in running the business, his son Charlie had taken over.
Warren Warehousing and Armysecure worked together when there was mutual opportunity, Armysecure had the

North and East covered with Warren Warehousing covering the Midlands and the West. Times were good and the cash was rolling in. This allowed Jacko to spend more time on his passion, the charity that Tommy had founded New Drill. The premise was simple, prevention and correction.

Every serviceman had access to New Drill. They ran courses on the transition from forces life to civvy life; simple things like how to rent a house, paying bills, getting mortgages. They held job fairs for leavers, often matching skills learnt in the forces with those required in civilian life, along with support for those men and women that suffered physical and mental illnesses. Those unfortunates were often pensioned out of the services and forgotten about by the government, the same government that was happy for them to lay down their lives.

The correction side of the charity, was working hand in hand with local authorities. Taking men and women off the street into half way homes, helping them deal with, and become part of, life outside of the forces. New Drill was, on the whole, staffed by ex-squaddies. Who better to help a soldier than a soldier?

Jacko now spent three days a week working for New Drill. Not taking a wage and helping wherever he was told he was most needed, quite often this was helping the soldiers that had ended up on the street.

"If the government won't look after you son, we will," he told an ex-Marine.

Tommy still had the computer and games shop. He had reluctantly stopped selling mobile phones when the market was flooded, with companies offering cut price phones along with contracts. The shop flourished and Jeff was practically an administrator, only occasionally spending time on the shop floor. Eggy continued to look after the geeks, as they were now known throughout the business, with the shop being staffed by knowledgeable young men and women that had a passion for computers and gaming.

50

Terry floated across Titanium's headquarters, visiting customers, spending time at the shop and anything else that Tommy wanted him to do. His role was one of trouble shooter and innovator. He was also a little different.
One Monday morning, when walking to his office, Tommy heard a strange tooting noise coming from the board room. When he looked in, Terry was sat with a phone in front of him, blowing notes into it from a penny whistle.
"I can't wait to hear this." said Tommy.
"Captain Crunch," came the reply.
Tommy sighed, entered the room, sat down and asked Terry to explain.
"OK, computers are pretty much infallible, unless they break, they do the same things all of the time. They respond to commands from software and hardware. Captain Crunch hacked into the US phone systems."
"Stop a sec, what the fuck is hacked?"
"Hacking is understanding how a computer works and changing the data to make it better. It is also fooling the system. John Draper, an American, is known as Captain Crunch because he found out, that by blowing a free toy whistle, out of a packet of Captain Crunch breakfast cereal, he could fool the phone companies into giving him free calls. I'm trying to get an outside line instead of dialling 9, like we normally do."
"And this will help us how?"
"It won't, but it's the principal. Most small businesses now have computers and all large businesses do. If we can hack into, say a rivals business, it would give us commercial advantages. Imagine knowing what a rival

warehouse was tendering for a contract, we could go in and win it or not spend time on it, if they were too cheap. I read in a magazine, that email services may become commonplace and not tied to service providers. Soon, that could lead to all sorts of opportunities, but we need to be the first. If we are second, we will be too late. I need to understand hacking and how to do it. I was going to come speak to you about this. Can I have a budget for two more employees and an office, away from here?"

Tommy sat thinking for a moment.

"It would be really useful to be able to spy on the opposition from within, I will give you that. How much do you want to pay these people?"

I have to find them yet. I want young, angry, talented people. It aint going to be easy but it's such an opportunity."

"OK, I have a shop that the occupier will be leaving when they end their lease. Come back to me, when you have more than tin whistles and maybes."

"Oh, I will, trust me. Honest to God Tommy, this will be huge, and it was a red plastic whistle."

51

In March of 1996, Terry asked Tommy and Jacko to join him in the boardroom, to meet someone called Cracker. Cracker was at a computer workstation and he looked like a typical student, scruffy denims and just a hint of fuck you in his demeanour.

"Tommy, Jacko, this is Cracker. I want you to watch as he demonstrates something.

In 10 minutes' time, the Tynetimes radio win a ticket phone in begins. They are offering up four tickets for the Newcastle Sunderland match this Saturday, it's an all expenses luxury box at St James. What happens is, the disc jockey gives out a number from one to a hundred, say its number thirty. The thirtieth caller to the station, win's the tickets. It's totally random, pot luck, but Cracker will make sure it is me. If you look at his screen, he has accessed the radio station network. Whenever I dial in, as long as it is before the winner has been spoken to, I will win the prize. Cracker will stall the system, until he can see my call, then place it in the right call order to be the 30th. Anyone, with the right talents, can get into a system as basic as this and Cracker is the best I have come across locally. Right here we go."

For the next couple of minutes, the four men in the room listened to the DJ talk up the prize, he then gave the radio phone number, a drum roll and selected the number fifty eight. Terry called the number straight away,

"There you are," said Cracker "number 23. Now, lets hide your number and slow down the system at their end."

His hands flew across his keyboard and the calls slowed down. Instead of maybe 6 or 7 a minute, to 3 or 4. Each call was answered, the caller commiserated with and the

call was ended. Eventually the phone was hung up on number 57.
"Now we move you next in line." A couple of seconds later, a voice came onto Terry's phone.
"Tynetimes radio, how can I help you?"
"Four tickets to the match please," Terry replied.
The receptionist on the other end said, "please just wait a second," Terry was put on hold, then to a loud fanfare, he was talking to the Radio's DJ.
"Congratulations. You have just won yourself four tickets to the big game. What's your name?"

52

The following morning, Tommy, Jacko and Terry met again.

"I have to admit" said Tommy "that was impressive. Tell me about Cracker"

"He's 19 years old, a proper computer geek. Spends every free second he has, either stripping down computers or accessing networks. There are loads of kids like him out there. I chose him because he hasn't got some fuck you chip on his shoulder and his home life is shit. His dad is a piss head and free with his hands. If you want to take this further, he can come live with me and we will see how we get on. Right now, he is happy to come for a roof over his head and some tax free expenses. He wants to know what it would be like, before he comes on board with us, and I want to get to know him better."

"Where does he live now and how did you get to know him?"

"He lives in Thirsk. I met him at a computer fair, a few months ago. He is a top player on Nintendo. I bought him a coke and we had a chat. Since then, I have popped over once or twice a week and I'm sure as I can be, that he's trustworthy."

"What did he charge for yesterday's demonstration?"

"That was free. I have told him that he would need to dangle the carrot, if he was to stand a chance of working with us. I also told him, if he does, he will become part of a proper family. A team that looks out for one another and other people too, that really appealed to him."

"One thing from me" said Jacko. "What about Sally? How's she going to feel about you taking in super geek?"

"Me and Sally are about done. She keeps talking getting engaged, having kids. I'm too young for all of that, right now."

"Are you sure? She seems like a nice girl. Don't you want to settle down?"

"Perfectly sure. I'm just not ready for family life. If you're by yourself, you can't get hurt. Now moving on."

Jacko took the hint. "I think it's worth a try Tommy. Keep him distant from what we do, but let Terry spend more time with him. More time out of the office, in that shop, just the two of them. Let's see what they can come up with?"

"Agreed. You have Monday, Wednesday and Friday mornings with him. Give him £100 a week cash, I will set up an account you can draw it from. Tell him it's £120, if he smartens up, gets a haircut and a shave. The rest of the time he can help out the geeks. You know those guys pretty well, get some feedback from them too."

"Fantastic, I know he will be good for us. He's a little lost, has no clue about life. He just needs a cuddle and pointing in the right direction."

"OK, take the rest of the day off. Spend it with him, get him presentable and bring him in Monday morning. I want to get to know him a little."

"Cheers Tommy, see you Monday. Oh, and enjoy the match tomorrow."

On Monday morning, Tommy and Jacko sat in the board room, they were joined by Terry and Cracker.

Cracker had on a formal shirt, chinos and desert boots. His hair was cut short and he was clean shaven.

"Looking good Cracker," said Jacko.

"Thank you" Cracker replied, quietly.

"I have already told Cracker that he is amongst friends here. We have rules of course but as long as he does a day's work for us, is honest and trustworthy, he will be part of our family." said Terry.

"How was your weekend Cracker?" asked Tommy.

"Fine thank you Mr Flounders."

"First rule Cracker, I'm Tommy. This is Jacko and, of course, you know Terry. No Mr Flounders, Cracker. Well not unless I am shouting at you," he finished with a warm smile.

"Can I just say that the weekend was better than fine. Cracker here, only accessed the Dole office network and deleted all of his dad's records. When he goes to sign on, they will never have heard of him."

"It will take the bastard weeks to get some money," said Cracker.

"Right, that does sound impressive, but is it secure? We don't want the old bill lifting you. I am sure we can give you a good career but not if the law comes sniffing around," Tommy chipped in.

"I didn't leave any footprints and, to be honest Tommy, as far as I know there are no laws against what I have done. There are pretty much no laws at all, for the internet."

"OK, I will get the lawyers to check what legislation applies. Now tomorrow, Cracker, pack a bag. We will be heading off for a few days. I want to show you around the business Tuesday and Wednesday and Jacko will finish off Thursday Friday with New Deal our charity. This will give us all the chance to get to know each other better and if you see anything that you think you can improve, when we are out and about, shout up."

53

Tuesday morning came and Cracker was ready with his bag. Well, Terry's bag. After a hearty breakfast, served up in Tommy's favourite caff in Murray Street, they headed off on a two day tour of the warehouses that Armysecure had. Tommy explained how each one was run, how the chain of command worked and how records were kept, of which pallets belonging to which companies, were in which locations.
Cracker took particular interest on this.
"Would it help if we could keep all these records on computers, rather than have all of the paperwork you currently use?" he asked.
"It is something I have been thinking about for a while," Tommy replied. "There are systems out there, that would help but they are very expensive and I don't want outside agents accessing our information. Some of the storage we do is highly sensitive," he added cryptically.
Cracker was wise enough not to pursue that.
"I'm sure me and Terry could put together a robust spreadsheet system, to run alongside the paper system you have in place. The good thing about spreadsheets is that, with a click of a button, you can change the information you keep or even delete it, if you chose to."
'Cracker's reading between the lines,' thought Tommy. 'Good lad.'
"OK, well we will be meeting next week, after Jacko has explained what we do with New Drill. We can discuss what I want you and Terry to do then."
The two days with Jacko were spent understanding what New Drill offered, from basic half day training sessions to intervention for ex-servicemen that had fallen upon hard times. These were mainly drug or alcohol addicts, so intervention was costly and often fruitless.

"The vast majority of our funds come from Armysecure, Titanium Security and their customers. We have fund raising events in the services but to be honest, servicemen need every penny they earn, just to keep the wolf from the door."

"What's the website like?"

"It's ok. We have a page showing what we do and phone numbers to contact for help, and to contribute."

"OK then" said Cracker, hesitantly.

The following Monday, Tommy, Jacko, Andrew Leeson and Pudding Smithies met with Terry and Cracker, in the boardroom of Titanium Security.

"Right Cracker, what do you think of our little enterprise?" asked Tommy.

"It's 'ellish," came the reply.

"It may be 'ellish' son," chipped in Jacko "but as we are in the boardroom, shall we agree that it is brilliant. There is a very good chance you will be meeting customers in here, we need to sound professional not council estate."

"Yeah sorry, I understand, it is pretty good," said Cracker grinning.

"Christ, he's only been here 2 minutes and already he takes the piss, like super geek over there," Pudding Smithies added, nodding towards Terry.

"OK guys, enough now. Terry, when we were touring the warehouse, Cracker said you could do some sort of spreadsheet, to help us reduce the reliance on paperwork. Is that right?"

Terry replied "It should be pretty straight forward. We have been chatting about it at the weekend. There will be some investment in the infrastructure having computers at charge hand work stations, out in the warehouses. Some overnight backups to a central system, just in case we have a failure anywhere. We should be up and running in six to eight weeks, if you want to trial a customer at each warehouse? This will allow us to iron out any glitches and to give hands on training, for those that need it. You could, of course, rent a system but they are very expensive."

"Perfect, let's give it a trial run at Catterick and then if it's ok, filter it to all premises. If that's everything, Terry and Cracker, you can go make a start. The rest of us need to review current stockholdings and opportunities."

"There is one thing," said Cracker. "I have been looking at the New Drill website and it's pretty poor, to be honest. Can we look at improving that too?"

"No problems with that but remember, Armysecure pays the bills and supports New Drill, so that has to be the priority."

Within twelve weeks, all of the warehouses were beginning to convert a single client, to a very basic warehouse management system. Each pallet that arrived into the warehouse was issued a pallet number, that could be cross referenced by, customer, order number and part number, if needed. The put away location was also recorded. Using data that ran from a master spreadsheet, that Terry and Cracker had devised, the pallet could be searched for by pallet number, part number and order number.

The warehouse chargehands could search for empty pallet locations, for incoming stock and once customers called off pallets for despatch, they were picked and moved to holding locations, grouped by customer and van or lorry route.

The board met, to review the progress that Terry and Cracker had made with the warehouse systems. They agreed a cautious roll out, across all the customer base, whilst continuing to record manually, as a back up until all customers were on the new system and that Tommy was satisfied that the initial results were replicated.

"After all" he said, "the feedback from the shop floor is positive and if these guys like and use it, then we should be on a winner. Anything else before we wrap up?"
"Yes" said Terry. "Me 'n' Cracker have been working on a new website for New Drill. Can we show you?"
"Sure, go ahead," said Tommy.
The potential new website was warmly received by everyone around the table. Not only was it more eye catching than the last one, but it had a number of pages. One to detail how ex-servicemen could get in touch, with phone numbers by area and another showing the main contributors to the charity.
"We have put these in order of contributions made, but you can have them any way you want," said Cracker.
"We can also add case studies if you want, changing names obviously," chipped in Terry. "It seems like the bigger, the better with websites these days."
"This looks really good. When did you do all this?" asked Jacko.
"We done it over the last 6 weekends. It was hard work but good fun and we have learnt a hell of a lot," said Terry.
"Ok, any more for any more, before we finish?" Tommy paused. "Ok guys, thank you. Terry and Cracker, can you hang back please?"
The room quickly emptied. Jovial voices could be heard heading down to the canteen, where ribbing, sometimes vicious but never said with malice, would accompany coffee and a bacon buttie, before people headed off to complete the rest of the working day.

54

"Right guys, I was impressed with the with the warehouse stuff and the New Drill website is a significant improvement. Ranking companies by how much they have donated, is a great idea and, if we manage it well, we might be able to up the money we raise, with some friendly rivalry between some of our customers.
Cracker, you have had 3 months now. How do you feel about coming onto the books, full time?"
Crackers face split into a broad grin. "Thought you would never ask Tommy, but seriously, I feel like I have a purpose for the first time in my life. Those guys who work for you from the Army are so tight, like a big family. They don't know me from shit but all of them have been great. Every one of them, makes a point of speaking to me. I can't imagine working anywhere else. I don't want to blow smoke up Terry's arse either but he is a top man. Where do I sign?"
"I will have a contract drawn up over the next few days. As with Terry, I will be paying you more than you currently bring in to the company, but I know in my bones that computers, the internet and stuff to do with both, that I can't even imagine, will bring wealth, power and opportunity to anyone who is first to utilise it. I want us to be first.
Over the last few weeks, Terry has been feeding you a little more about our shadier side of the business. Along with the day to day computer and security arms of the group, I want you two to focus on what you can do to make money. Either by helping us stay one step ahead of the competition or by another way. The problem is, I don't know what that other way is, so you guys will have to find it for me.

Finally, I will budget for two more employees. I want these guys to be mavericks, to have a flair for what they do, just as you both have. You will need to be sure of them, be sure of their loyalty. There is no clock on this, finding the right people will take as long as it takes. Just be absolutely sure, before you bring them onboard.
I am taking a huge risk on you guys and the team you build. Risking the group of businesses and all the people who work here, every fucking thing! I am setting up a new company, Flounders and Partners Technologies. You guys are currently the only employees. As of the first of next month, you will sub-contract to the rest of the group. You will run as a standalone business.
I have secured a small administration unit for you, just around the corner. You will have full control over your time, when not subbying to me. I have never given anyone, this amount of autonomy. Don't let me down."
"Don't worry Tommy. We love this place and the people who work here. We won't risk it and we will make sure you are always, at least 2 steps, ahead of your competition," said Terry.
"Right guys. Go back to it and work out what you can do, how and eventually who with?"

55

Over the following 4 years, Tommy, Jacko, Andrew Leeson and Pudding Smithies consolidated the warehousing businesses and expanded the delivery service, to cover other warehouse chains along with their own. Titanium Security grew each year, with more and more ex-forces men coming into the job market, recruiting loyal hard working employees was never a problem for Tommy. New Drill was always a drain on resources and funds, but Tommy and especially Jacko donated lots of hours, outside of their working time to the charity. Their aim to ensure that every opportunity was given to people leaving the services, to have the right knowledge to compete in civvy street.

Flounders and Partners grew from Terry and Cracker, to a team of six young tech savvy people. None, other than Terry, had formal qualifications (and he was the butt of many jokes for this fact). All were exceptional at what they did. Not only were they hacking customers and rivals' emails and systems, but they also worked diligently to protect Tommy's group of businesses from any danger, including the infamous Love Bug Worm, that circulated in 2000. Originating in the Philippines, the worm affected an estimated 10% of all the worlds computers, that were attached to the internet. Flounders and Partners had a busy 2000, repairing infected computers and restoring corrupted files. On occasion copying files to their own servers, if it was thought it could give Tommy's group of companies a commercial advantage.

The team were exceptionally close. Cracker still lived at Terry's, with the remaining four sharing a six bedroom, three bathroom house that Tommy bought, on Station Lane, a stone's throw from Terry's house. They worked hard and when times were quiet, they visited every tech chat room, to keep in touch with shady figures across the globe. They were always looking to increase their knowledge and seek out opportunities, to either improve their current activity or identify new opportunities for the business, legal or otherwise. They were fiercely loyal to each other and to Tommy, whom they held in a god like regard.

'Christ!' thought Tommy, as he stretched his fingers for what seemed like the hundredth time, 'who would have thought that a handful of misfits, would eventually grow into one of the best group of people I have ever met. Three of them married now, seven kids between them and all of them loyal, to their very core. It's because of them, that I am lying under this fucking bush, waiting to deliver what's due, to a piece of scum that pollutes everywhere he walks and breathes.'

56

Clive Ness was through and through a service man. Joining the Royal Green Jackets at 18, he was physically fit and articulate. He worked well under pressure, was confident and friendly, able to give orders and act unquestionably when given orders. He excelled with a rifle and went on to specialise as a precision marksman (sniper). He was decorated for his service in Afghanistan and Iraq. He wasn't decorated or recognised for covert operations in Sudan and Syria, Eastern Europe and on one occasion, the USA. He was headhunted to the British secret service in 2014 and now carries out covert operations for the UK Government, anywhere across the world. Despite his talents, he is mainly desk bound, having worked his way up to a senior position, in his current placement. Because of this, he was quite surprised when tasked with the kill of a UK civilian. The orders coming through directly from the most senior man in his group.

He was given a date and approximate time of the mission, which in turn raised his eyebrows. He would be executing a man, immediately after the civvy had killed another man, both of them seemingly legitimate businessmen. Still orders were orders.

A few days before the execution of the mission, he scoped out the area that the killing would take place, noting where he thought the mark would park his car, where best to position himself and what weapons he would need. He chose an Accuracy-International produced L96A1 sniper rifle. The cartridge a 7.62 X 51mm NATO round, was probably a little overkill, but as kill was the name of the game, then why not! For a side arm, he had selected the Dan Wesson DWX loaded with 19 rounds of 9mm 115 grain full metal jacket cartridges.

He certainly would not need the Wesson for the kill, but it might be needed if he encountered civilians, immediately after the kill.

Arriving to carry out the mission, he was pleased to note that the marks car was parked where he had suspected it would be. Some 40 meters from where Ness had parked his own transport. Ness assumed, correctly, that the mark would make his way through a wooded area. It was covered in heavy bushes but navigable, to the property boundary where the mark would then cross a well kept lawn and hide in bushes, close to the main house, where the targets car was kept.

Ness found a perfect spot to lay low, until the target cleared the bushes at the side of the property and began to make his way across the grass, directly towards where Ness was waiting.

'Thomas Flounders,' Ness thought to himself. 'I have no idea what you have done but, by fuck, you have upset the wrong people.' Ness rarely cared about who or why, but in this instance, as it was a UK civilian, Ness had conducted a few discreet searches. Flounders, a business man based in Hartlepool, was a driving force behind New Deal, a charity for ex-service personnel. It seemed a shame that Flounders was to be killed but there must be a good reason for it, and after all despite Flounders perfect record, he was here to kill someone himself.

Ness settled down, rolling in the dirt, to make sure when the time came, there would be no intrusive roots or branches that would put him off his shot. His rifle on the ground, Ness practised rolling into position. Picking up the rifle, siting the scopes until he was perfectly happy. He rested the rifle to his right hand side, made himself as comfortable as possible and waited.

Ness prided himself in working alone and acting decisively. The mission he was on, was as straight forward as it came. Rifle shots were notoriously difficult to pinpoint by sound alone. In almost all terrain, the noise tended to reverberate and appear to come from several places at once. It is unlikely that anyone, other than a former service man, would even recognise the rifle shot for what it was. Ness would be away and in traffic, probably on the A1 if not further South and across onto the M1, before police arrived on the scene. The cartridge would be collected, with no trace of him left, other than the body of a man missing most of his head.

57

The years following the millennium passed quickly for Tommy. Flounders and Partners flourished. Terry and Cracker, or William as his business cards had printed on them, drove the business forwards. They worked hard to find young tech savvy young people. Chatting to them for months, in online forums, sharing hacking techniques. Deciding which of them, they thought, were suitable to their business. Every time they invited someone up to the office for a week, it was a risk but so far, not one of the additional four people they had recruited had left the team. They all showed remarkable loyalty, dealing with the day to day contracting to Titanium Securities, whose own computer services side of the business, had grown significantly quicker that the physical security side of the business.

Despite Titanium keeping them busy, the main role for Terry, Cracker and the team, was the shadier side of the internet. They were regularly able to crack customers, suppliers and competitor's computer and email systems, keeping Tommy one step ahead of the field and enabling the warehousing side of the business to stand its own, in an increasingly tough environment.

The introduction of broadband, from the year 2000, had transformed what the guys were able to do.

Many senior business computer users, were in position where a handshake and contract was all that was needed. They still considered fax machines as cutting edge. A significant number of these senior personnel, distrusted and disliked computers and emails. They let their ignorance, override the very basic training they had been given, in computer security. Many still used 'password' for their email and personal passwords. Once Terry and Cracker had an email address, it was normally only minutes before inboxes and stored documents were copied and saved to a Flounders and Partners server. Tommy and his businesses used this to their advantage, by either negotiating the best deal possible, based on their rivals bids, or being aware of financial difficulties of a customer / potential customer and acting accordingly. Andrew Leeson and Pudding Smithies both had a small team of hand picked men. Men that were able to deal with the complexities of the business they worked for, but more importantly, men that were prepared to bend or clearly break the law, if they were ever called on. The links between Tommy's group of companies and New Drill were common knowledge, with many service men seeking their help or positions within Tommy's group of businesses, before leaving the forces.

58

Despite the commercial advantage Tommy had over his rivals, it was decided in 2015 by the senior board, that due to pressure from bigger warehouse chains, Armysecure would be put up to tender. Despite having eyes and ears in most of Tommy's warehouse business rivals, the bigger businesses were prepared to run at a loss to secure new contracts and put other groups out of operation. They operated globally and offered an end to end supply chain and logistic package, that Tommy couldn't match. Tommy was able to negotiate a favourable deal, ensuring Armysecure would retain its identity for 3 years and continue to staff at least 35% of it's labour from ex-service personnel, for the next 5 years.

When the Warehouse group was sold in 2016, all the board members became wealthy men, as not only the warehouses and current contracts were sold but also the freehold of the properties and these had increased in value significantly over the years, Tommy had always rewarded those who he worked close to, with shares in his businesses, reasoning loyalty doesn't pay the bills and he himself only needs so much money.

The bulk of the revenue from the sale, was put into a trust, to maintain New Drill for the following 5 years although donations from local businesses remained high, mainly due to Jacko, Pudding and Andrew driving the fund-raising side of the charity.

"That's it then," said Tommy at the board meeting. He looked around the table, as always Jacko sat at the opposite end of the table to Tommy, he was flanked either side by Pudding Smithies and Andrew Leeson. Terry sat to Tommy's left, with Cracker, the newest and most junior board member, to Tommy's right. "All of you could now retire and live a life of luxury if you choose to do so. The money you have made, from the sale of the warehouses is significant. All I need to know is, do any of you want to leave?"

The no's from around the table were unanimous and vocal.

"What I want to do," Tommy continued, "is to continue with the distribution side of the business. We still have an edge there and can make a good margin. Titanium Security is our main growth opportunity, subcontracting security and of course, internet safety. Flounders and Partners will continue to offer support, as and when called upon.

I have been working on a project with Terry and Cracker for a number of months now. I don't know if you guys have heard of Bitcoin? It has been around for about 6 years. Please don't ask me to explain it. Terry and Cracker have tried to explain it to me, half a dozen times, and I still can't grasp it, but this allows us to basically tax businesses, pretty much anonymously. Back in the day, I would do a tax run every Monday, picking up cash from a number of places across Hartlepool, to ensure their insurance and safety. We plan to do the same to businesses across the UK, and maybe even further afield, but instead of a weekly tax we will visit them once, corrupt their computer systems and restore them for a fee, paid in bitcoins, which can then be converted to real cash, as and when we choose. Terry, Cracker and me will be the main beneficiaries but you guys will also do well from it, as will New Deal. There may be times, when we need a little muscle but I don't think this will be too often.

A sideline of this, will be identifying the occasional front business for criminal gangs and deciding, based upon their activities, if we need to take them down. This is

where you three," Tommy nodded towards the other end of the table, "will run the show. So now you know the plan. Are you guys all still in?"
There were no changes. Everyone was keen and curious about Tommy's new enterprise.
"Good stuff. There should be bacon butties in the canteen. Let's get down there before they get cold."

59

On the 6th August 2016 at 2.30am, Jacko made his bed, showered, dressed and checked the five envelopes that were laid out on the kitchen table. He left his house, locking it behind him.
It was a warm morning with the sound of the waves, crashing onto Seaton Carew beach, accompanying his walk. Jacko made his way along Warrior Drive, turning right into Queen Street, he didn't dawdle but nor was he rushing, He turned left into Lawson Road and followed it until it met Marine Drive. He crossed over the road and followed the promenade past Tommy's house and on to the slipway to the beach, opposite the Staincliffe Hotel. He walked down to the beach, settling himself into the damp sand. He lit a cigarette, the first in over 20 years and after a little coughing, he took his mobile phone from his pocket and dialled 999.
"Emergency services, which service please?"
"Police and ambulance please" Jacko replied.
"Could you tell me the nature of the incident?" the responder asked.
"My name is Jacko. I am sat at the bottom right of the slipway, outside of the Staincliffe Hotel, Seaton Carew, Hartlepool. I have a LA91 9mm Browning Pistol and am going to commit suicide. I would like the police on hand, so that I am not discovered by a civilian."
"Please just give me one moment sir." The call centre operator immediately notified his supervisor of the situation, who in turn called both the police and ambulance services. "I'm just going to transfer you to one of my colleagues," the operator said.
A second later, a new voice spoke to Jacko. "Hi I'm Tim. Are you Jacko?"
"Hello Tim, you must be the trained negotiator, are you?"

"Yes I guess you could put it like that. Would you like to tell me what's going on? I am sure there must be something we can do about it."

"Tim, can you tell me, are the police and ambulance service on the way?"

"Yes sir, they should be with you shortly."

"Good. Now I know enough, to know you will try to engage me, to try to talk me out of what I am doing but I would be really grateful if you wouldn't. I have been diagnosed with dementia; I have had a second opinion which confirms the first. I have no family, but friends that are close enough, to put their own lives on hold for however many years it takes me to die. I have served in Her Majesty's armed forces. Since leaving the Army, I have had a successful career in civvy street. There is no way in a million years that I am going to allow myself to drift into a world, where I become a burden to others. Where I end up in a goddamn care home, sat dribbling into my lap, wearing nappies and not recognising people I love. You understand that, Tim?"

"Yes Jacko, I do, but surely you have a good few years in you yet?"

"I might do Tim, but after the good few years, I might just have a couple of not bad years, followed by years and years of oblivion. By doing this now, I am in control of my life, something I value greatly. Now I did ask you not to try to talk me out of this. Should I hang up or would you rather just talk shit to me?"

"Shit it is then Jacko. It looks like the police will reach you first and they should be with you in around 10 to 15 minutes. You said you have very close friends. Do you want to tell me about them?"

"Tim I know literally hundreds of people and, up until around fifteen weeks ago, I knew everyone of them by name and something about each of them, something that is important to them. Now those memories are slipping out of my grasp, only frustration where once a name sat. There are two guys, Tommy and Terry, Tommy is like a brother to me I would lay down my life for him, every second I breathe, and I know he would do the same for me. Terry is the son I never had. A bright, witty, good looking, fit young man who is a credit to his mother. Again I would die for him and vice versa. I love these guys. There are others, Pudding and Andrew, such great mates, and colleagues. I have lived a life rich with adventure, achievement, and friendship. I lived it on my terms and leave it the same. Now where the fuck are the bizzies Tim?"

"Only a couple of minutes now Jacko. It sounds like you could write a book about your life."

Jacko chuckled. "There's no way I could do that Tim, way too many skeletons. Women I have bedded that I shouldn't, deeds done honourable and otherwise but all justifiable in front of God. My book would be full of omissions, but those who know my life may write one for me one day. Who knows? Those who are closest to me, will be angry that I have chosen the path I have but they will also understand. Tim, our time is done. I can see the blue flashing lights. Thank you for your time tonight, be sure I will not forget your name, for as long as I live."

Moments later, a young police officer shone a torch down from the promenade, picking up Jacko on the beach.

"Sir, give me a moment. I will come down to see you, see if we can't sort something out."

"Just listen one second son, to my right is a large envelope with all the details you need. The pistol I have with me has only one round in it. The remaining ammunition will be found in my garage, in a steel toolbox, that sits in the middle of the floor. I know you will need to search the property but that toolbox with be the only thing of interest to you."

With that said, Jacko lay on his left side using his right hand he held the pistol to his head. The barrel resting behind his ear, taking care to make sure the bullet would pass through his brain and not out through his face. Jacko thought of his best mate and whispered, "sorry" and pulled the trigger ending his life.

60

The knock on Tommys door, came around 10:30 that morning. He was aware that something was going on across the road. Two police vans were parked on the promenade and the access to the beach was taped off. He was surprised to see Assistant Chief Constable, Chris Kaine, on his doorstep, Tommy still donated regularly to the local police force charities and knew the Assistant Chief on a first name basis.
"Chris, what brings you here on a Saturday morning. Is everything ok?"
"Can I come in Tommy"
"Sure, follow me." As much as Tommy knew Chris, he still had a deep mistrust of the Police. He led Chris into his kitchen. "Can I get you a cuppa and you can tell me why you are here?"
"No thank you Tommy. I will be brief. This morning, a little after 3am, John Jackson, Jacko took his own life across the road. He told the call centre operative he chatted to, before killing himself, that he had been diagnosed with dementia and that he did not want to be a burden on his close friends. I guess that means you, in particular.
We are in the process of conducting a search of his house, as he used a firearm but have already recovered what he told us are the only munitions on the property. We have also secured five envelopes, one for his solicitor and four others addressed to yourself, someone called Terry, the staff at your offices and the bar at Catterick army camp. I see no reason to hold onto these Tommy, so here you are." He laid the envelopes on the kitchen island. "Can I do anything at all for you?"
"Fucking hell Chris. Fucks sake, I never had a clue! No thank you, please let yourself out."

As the front door closed, Tommy sat at a kitchen chair and cried, as hard as he did when Julie died.
It was an hour later, before he could muster the courage, to open the envelope addressed to himself.

61

'Brother I am sorry I had to do this to you, but I love you too much, to ask you to watch me die slowly. Please don't be angry with me, for not telling you what was going on. I know if I had told you, you would have found some way to talk me out of doing this. I couldn't let that happen.
I have loved working with you, I am honoured to call you a friend. Since I came to work with you, I have felt nothing but joy. My life has been full and rewarding. I didn't want to end, not knowing what we have achieved, sat in a room somewhere, with no understanding of my life.
Some might say, it's a cowards way out but I think you know me well enough to know, I see it as a honourable way to go.
Please look after Terry. I know you think of him as a son, and so do I. He will be hurting. He's had enough loss in his life and now I add to it.
I have left something to you and Terry in my will. Pretty much every other penny to my name will go to New Drill. I know in my heart, we have saved lives. If you do anything, in remembrance of me, keep New Drill going. If this country won't look after its ex-servicemen, we will have to.
Tommy Flounders, brother, colleague, friend. I am honoured to have known you.'
Tommy put the handwritten letter down on the dining room table. He had read it time after time, since Chris Kaine left. For 3 hours, he had drunk coffee, read the letter and cried. He sighed. 'Well I had better start sorting this shit show out. Damn Jacko, you could have let me say goodbye' he thought to himself.

62

Terry picked up the call on the third ring. "Yo Tommy are we out for a beer?"
"Later on, maybe, but I need you and Cracker round mine, as soon as you can."
"OK Tommy, it sounds serious. What's up?"
"Just get here."
An hour later, Tommy, Terry and Cracker sat in the spacious living room overlooking the sea front. Terry had cried, then cried again, when he read his letter. Jacko had told Terry that he considered him to be his son, and that a father could not be prouder of his boy than Jacko was of Terry. He told him much the same as he had told Tommy but begged Terry, to make sure that Tommy was alright. 'You know how he keeps his emotion in check, how he never shows weakness. He's going to be hurting too son, but he won't show it. Make sure you spend time with him.'
Cracker was inconsolable, he had sobbed, showing real grief.
"Why the fucking hell did he do it? He could have talked to us, we could have got nurses, anything he needed. There was no need to kill himself. He is such a good guy. He always knew what to say. Why the fuck has he died?"
"He did what he thought best Cracker. I don't think there's a man we know, who would want to go out not knowing who he was, not being able to communicate and wearing nappies. I'm gutted son, more than you could ever imagine but I understand why he did it. From now on, whatever we do, whatever we risk, we do it in honour of Jacko. That is the finest tribute we could pay, to one of the best friends, a man could ever have.

I have to phone Pudding and Andrew. After that, I will prepare a brief which will sit alongside Jacko's letter to everyone who works with us. All of us on the senior team, will need to make ourselves available to anyone who needs to talk. We also have to make sure we can pretty much shut our businesses, on the day of the funeral.

I would imagine the coroner will release the body soon enough. On Monday, I will start arranging the funeral and meet with his solicitor. If you guys want to go buy some beers and a decent bottle of brandy, we can toast him tonight. I have beds made up. Tonight we laugh, cry, get drunk and celebrate our mate."

63

The next two weeks passed so quickly for Tommy and his closest friends and colleagues.
Via his solicitor, Jacko had requested a cremation, with his ashes to be scattered in Hartlepool bay. Tommy had briefed as many people as he could personally, even visiting the warehouses that still bore his company name at shift changeovers. Word had spread quickly with so many men and women shocked and saddened at Jacko's death.
The letters that Jacko had left for Titanium and New Deal personnel were brief. He told everyone how proud he was to have been part of their lives and ask that they remember him favourably, as a colleague, and not to linger on his way of passing.
Fittingly, it was an overcast day on the day of the funeral. There was standing room only at the crematorium, with more than a 100 outside. The wake was held at the Staincliffe Hotel. Jacko had left £5000 to pay for food and drink. Within hours, the Staincliffe had been drunk dry. Squaddies, ex-squaddies, civilians, all sharing stories and anecdotes, as the day drifted into night. A bonfire was built on the beach, close to where Jacko had died. Taxis were taken to supermarkets, then filled with booze and snacks. It had been a long, long day for Tommy. He was stone cold sober, spending time with anyone who wanted to talk to him.
On the following Saturday, Tommy and the remaining members of the board along with other close friends, went to Catterick barracks, to give Jacko his final send off, from where he was perhaps most comfortable. The bar was rammed, from the moment it opened, and despite strict regulations, it did not shut that night. Tommy footed the bill and included dozens of take away

deliveries, that were spread amongst the drunk squaddies. As daylight broke, Tommy, Terry and Cracker made their way to a vacant house, that had been furnished with cots for them by the camp commander.

With coffees brewed, Tommy said "Tomorrow the board is meeting. Life must go on. It has changed forever but it will go on. Everything we do now, we do to honour our friend. Right let's get some fucking kip."

64

The following morning, at 11am precisely, an extraordinary board meeting was convened. Jacko's normal place at the table was left empty, that chair would never be sat in again, by either employee or guest. In time, Tommy would have a small brass name plate made, that simply read 'Jacko, here in spirit.' He would place it on the table in front of the empty chair.
"Right guys, I know that none of us have finished grieving and I'm not sure we ever will. That's fine, I wouldn't have it any other way, but life has to go on. So firstly, with what has happened, do any of you want to either retire or step back to a less demanding role, so that you can spend more time with friends and family? I know you guys all work hard but now's your chance to change that. I am going to keep on driving the businesses forwards. It's all I know to do. It's the only way I can cope, but I only want you guys to be here, if you really want to be."
The men around the table were unanimous in their desire to keep working with Tommy. Many still had questions about Jacko, anecdotes they wanted to share, but all realised that this was neither the time or place, this was business.
"Thank you, gentlemen that means a lot. I have been named by Jacko, as an executor of his will. I will be meeting with his solicitor this afternoon. He has left me his medals and Terry a few other personal items. Sanderson's will be clearing his house on Friday. If any of you want a memento of Jacko, I will be there on Thursday from about three. Just pop in, wander around and grab what takes your fancy, The house will be going up for sale on Monday. All of Jacko's estate will be going to New Drill. I have decided, that whatever Jacko would

have earned, will be transferred on a monthly basis to New Drill. I will do everything I can, to drive the charity forwards. This will be Jacko's legacy. OK, any questions or comments?"

"Wouldn't have it any other way" Pudding said, quietly.

"Good, now Terry and Cracker, you need to keep driving Flounders and Partners, both legitimate and otherwise. Terry, I am also putting you in my place, working with the senior team of Titanium security. The manual security side will still be managed by Andrew and Pudding, but I need you two to see what you can drive with the cyber security side. We have a good reputation with our customers, but need more exposure. So that's your task. I will be stepping back from my day to day role at Titanium, to allow me to focus more time with New Drill. I will still play an active part in all of the companies, and will be available for strategy and full senior team meetings, but will let go of the day to day unless you guy's call upon me. I also want you two," Tommy nodded towards Pudding and Andrew "to find a couple of guy's each. Guys you would trust with your life, who can support both sides of our enterprise, legal and otherwise. Other than that, it's business as usual or as usual as it can be. Any questions?"

"I was just wondering, how everything was going with the bitcoin thing?" Pudding said.

"Terry, Cracker, can you boys brief on the progress?" replied Tommy.

Terry and Cracker explained that they had been mimicking companies, that used standard cyber security protocols and off the shelf protection. Then looking for ways to breach them, quietly (without the target realising) and noisily, when using hacking techniques to disable software in company systems. In reality, with a real company, this would mean that we could then demand a payment, in bitcoin, which is pretty much untraceable, to reinstate the companies systems.

"So far so good," said Cracker. "We are pretty much good to go. The idea is, we check out a company, see how well it is doing? What their cash reserves are, how kosher it is. Then if all is good, we break their systems, demand a payment and if they comply then we take the money, remove our software and leave them to it. We will only target companies that have larger businesses behind them. We will not hurt growing start ups, just established cash rich companies. We actually have the first business identified. We are in and having a look around. If all goes to plan, we will be briefing you guys next week and doing this for real."

"You're sure about security. This won't come back to us?" asked Andrew.

"Absolutely. We have some of the best in the game working with us. We are watertight." Terry replied, "but should the worst come to the worst, we will be a group of geeks, acting alone."

"Right then lads. I look forwards to next week, with some anticipation. I could do with a little risk in my life. If there's nothing else, let's get downstairs for a sarnie and a brew in the canteen. We can't pretend nothing has happened but we have to show, life goes on. Try to get the balance right boys." Tommy said, standing up and finishing the meeting.

65

Clive Ness' phone rang unexpectedly. His watch told him it was a withheld number but he would have expected that. Live missions like this, were often subject to change or updated information and a withheld number cannot be extracted from a phone's software, if it should fall into the wrong hands. He had an earpiece and microphone as standard equipment.
"Ness." He answered.
"Captain Ness, my name is Pudding. I have a friend with me Andrew. It's really important you listen to what I have to say. The very first thing is, no sudden movements. Your life depends upon this. I also want to assure you, that if you comply, you will come to no harm whatsoever. We cannot allow you to carry out today's mission, but we do want to explain to you why."
'Compromised,' thought Ness.
"If you look forwards and to the base of the fir tree on your right, you will see two laser sighting marks appear. We will not hesitate to kill you if we must, we are ex-army too. Please just do exactly as I tell you.
We would like to make this as painless as possible. To do this, we must have your word, as an ex-colleague of the British armed forces, not to resist. We will have to relieve you of your weapons and search you. At times you will be hooded and restrained, but you will remain unharmed and released, once debriefed. You know what our colleague, Tommy, is here for today. So you can understand the implications, should you refuse to comply."
"I'm not sure I can trust two men that have pistols aimed at my back but in the circumstances I have no option but to agree," replied Ness.

"Good man. Now firstly, with your right hand, please push the rifle away from you using the stock." Ness complied. "Now tell me what side arms do you have?"

"A pistol holstered to my right hip."

"I am going to throw you a hood, please put it over your head using your right hand." Ness complied. "Put your hands behind your back. Now more than ever, it is important that you move slowly and do exactly as I say. We will tie wrap your wrists, relieve you of your weapons and search you."

Ness did exactly as he was asked, his hands were secured, he was relieved of his sidearm, a bunch of keys and his phone. Pudding made a call and still wearing his hood, Ness was guided to the edge of the copse.

Pudding made another call and within two minutes, a Transit van pulled immediately behind Ness' Mondeo. Ness was helped into the back of the Transit, the hood was removed and he was instructed to remove all his clothing. He was provided with fresh clean underwear, lounge wear and should he want it, a fleece. All of his clothing, his phone with the sim card removed and both weapons, were loaded into the boot of Ness' Mondeo, it was driven away by one of Puddings right hand men, and parked in a village hall car park, that was regularly used by visitors to the village for overnight parking. Tom (the driver of Ness' car) was picked up by a different car and the job was done.

"What happens now?" asked Ness, as the van began it's journey.

Andrew Leeson replied, "as we have said, we are removing you away for debriefing. In fact, it is more of a briefing than a debriefing. For the most part, it will be your target Tommy that talks to you. We have around a two and a half hour journey. If you want a drink, we have water and coffee, army coffee, hot strong and fucking awful. If you want a piss hold it or piss yourself."

"How did you guys know where I was? What I was about?"

"Again, the boss will tell you everything you want to know, within reason. For now, let's just say we got lazy, then we wised up, your team got lazy, now we hope to wise you up, but for now enough with the questions."

66

John Jameson enjoyed a leisurely shower. He felt on top of the world, 'not bad for a lad from a poor town in Yorkshire,' he thought to himself, as he looked around the spacious ensuite, in the rented property. John owned a lot of property, mainly two up two down, run down houses in the bad side of the towns he invested in. 'It's always easier to keep the poor in line than it is people with money, they believe in rights. The poor, well, they just want to survive day to day. If you have them down, keep them down,' he thought to himself.

John had a number of legitimate businesses but all were somehow linked to his illegitimate ones. The bars and clubs he owned, were ideal for laundering some of the drug's money he made. The massage parlours and strip joints did the same thing for the whores he ran. The rented houses went hand in hand with the loan sharking. The only problem he had right now, was the money was coming in so fast, he couldn't wash it all himself. He hated doing it but he had to use third parties for some of his cash flow. Losing 25% on the £ was criminal. 'Christ that's ironic,' he thought to himself. 'Me complaining about a criminal!' Business was booming and he needed to transfer some of the cash, which was now literally a garage full, through a number of transactions and finally back to his more legitimate businesses. He paid his taxes, kept a low profile, paid off coppers, distanced himself from any violence and was happy that he could live the life he chose, for as long as he wanted to.

Three years ago, business had boomed. A contact had asked if he could get a boat load of people across the channel and house them for a short time. Keen to take a chance with any opportunity and aware that people smuggling had become very lucrative, he purchased a seagoing semi-rigid inflatable power boat and opposed to the general rule, the boat travelled from the UK to France. It collected 28 people, mainly young men but some women and children with them, and brought them over to the UK. They travelled to Lincolnshire in a rigid sided 18 tonne lorry and were housed in a rundown but secure barn, John owned.

Within weeks, and after several more journeys, he had enough knowledge to make direct contact with the pitiful unfortunates that were desperate for a safer, more prosperous life in the UK, rather than use third parties as he had previously. He charged them up to £8k each for the short trip across the channel. Wherever possible, he picked up women and children. If they were accompanied by husbands, they were separated when they docked in the UK, with a promise they would be reunited shortly after.

John, however, had other ideas for some of those whom he trafficked. Children of both sexes, from the age of 3 onwards, were rented out or on occasion sold to the perverts that liked kids. Teenage girls and young women were put to work in John's brothels, to pay off their debt. The problem for them, they never quite earned enough to settle the debt.

John also made movies, any age, any activity. For sale on the dark web or on occasion, tailor made for the real sickos. The husbands and young men were sold to gang bosses. What the fuck they did with them John didn't care. He never looked at people as human beings but simply as assets, opportunities, tools to be used. When the tool was too fucked to be any use to him, he could always turn a few quid popping out a snuff movie.

The websites could be problematic. Only a few months ago, someone had hacked into the servers. They never got very far, or so John thought, but his IT guys had to spend a boat load of cash trying to make his servers more secure. He was sure there were better guys out there, to run his websites but the problem was, the product he was selling. He had to rely on a particular type of specialist, one that enjoyed the merchandise but because of that, they were not always the most knowledgeable.

'So here I am,' he thought, 'renting a fucking mansion not far from Castle Howard, a fucking Aston Martin in the garage, a Range Rover Autobiography on the drive if I needed it and a BMW M3 convertible, for Tanya to run around in.

Fucking Tanya, her days may be numbered,' he thought to himself. 'She's a good girl, fucks like a trooper, cooks well, looks good on the arm and knows how to take a slap when I lose my temper with her, but she snorts too much fucking coke, and its beginning to show.' She was so shitfaced last night, she back chatted him. He dealt with her swiftly. Gave her the biggest beating she had ever had from him. 'She won't be going anywhere for a week or so, until her face has healed up a little, but her days are numbered. Maybe I should make her a movie star,' he thought to himself.

John kept a Syrian girl in a whore house in Leeds, 15 years old and absolutely stunning. She was for him only and not to be rented out. She despised him and tried to fight him off every time, which was a bit of a turn on. He loved a bit of slap with his tickle. This bitch fought like a demon. She was, of course, no match for him but it always turned him on forcing her, seeing her break as he began to fuck her. Shit, he would probably pay her a visit tonight.

Dressed and looking sharp, he had a quick coffee in the kitchen before heading out of the front door and around to the triple sized garage at the right-hand side of the main house. It was still dark on the North Yorkshire landscape but motion action security lights helped him navigate his way quickly to the side of the building. He could see the garage from here and hit the auto door button, which moved up quickly and smoothly. 'Another day, another fucking dollar,' he thought to himself, as he walked towards the opening garage door.

The garage door began to move before Tommy heard John Jameson approaching. The spot light above the garage turned on dazzlingly bright and Tommy knew it would partially blind John, as he approached the garage. Tommy was a stickler for preparation. He had planned to shoot John Jameson immediately he passed the place where Tommy crouched. But the opportunity to shoot him as he entered the garage, apply the coup de grace and close the garage door behind him, hiding John's body, was too good to miss. The shot would only be a further 8 or 10 feet. Nothing for Tommy, who still shot regularly at Catterick barracks.

Tommy heard Johns leisurely approach on the sharp gravel, that flanked the house to the garage. Within seconds, he was level with Tommy, then past him. No faltering step that might alarm Tommy. John walked on, with not a care in the world. As he reached the garage entrance, Tommy raised his pistol.

John thought he had stumbled, but the way he fell, unable to break his fall with his arms, set alarm bells ringing. He tried to jump up, but nothing. He tried to call out but simply spat a glob of blood from his mouth. He heard footsteps approaching.

'Fuck,' was the last thing he ever thought.

Tommy shot John Jameson in the back of his head. The pistol shot reverberating louder than he would have liked. By John Jameson's right hand, a set of keys rested on the cold concrete floor. Tommy picked them up and found the garage door fob. He pressed the close icon and walked towards the end of the bushes and his planned escape route. He had taken the call from Pudding a while ago, to say that the second part of the plan had gone off perfectly. Still too dark to run, Tommy walked swiftly across the manicured lawn. He made his way quickly through the copse and on to his parked car. 'That's the simple bit done,' he thought to himself. The more challenging part of the operation, would unfold over the coming hours.

67

Tanya Murphy was in a world of pain with one eye swollen and both lips cut. She lay in bed, wondering how the fuck she got into this hole and more importantly, how the fuck she would get out? She had known all about John Jameson, even before he ever took interest in her. She knew he was crooked but had no idea how bad he was, until he had his claws deep into her. She was always a sucker for nose candy, she loved the high it gave her and John supplied as much as she could shovel up her nose. Once she had moved in with him, he began to treat her like a possession, she made excuses for him, of course. Girls like her always did, for men like him. He started just by giving her the odd slap, nothing more than a little bruising and normally where it would not be seen. More recently, he had become vicious, taking pleasure in hurting her. Taking his time, taunting her about how he was going to hit her, before he did. She heard the front door close. 'Thank fuck he's gone,' she thought to herself, wishing at the same time it would be that simple for her. Just open the door and drive away, but the reality was, she couldn't. He owned her. Tanya was no gangster but she recognised the gun shot for what it was. She held her breath and, before she exhaled, she heard a second shot. She pulled back the bedroom curtain just a fraction and saw a tall, lean man start to walk across the lawn, towards the trees and the road beyond.

Tanya realised immediately what had happened, and that this was her opportunity. This was the only chance she would ever get, not to rid herself of John, the mystery man had done that for her, but to get away with enough to make a fresh life for herself. Maybe moving

down to Cornwall, where her mum had retired to from Essex.
Wrapped in a robe she wandered downstairs poured a cup of coffee that she couldn't drink due to her broken lips and sat down to think.
Within an hour, she had taken £15,000 in cash and more importantly, a small velvet bag of diamonds, from John's floor safe, leaving £10,000 behind for the cops to find. He had showed her the diamonds one day and boasted there was over £150,000 worth in the bag. More than enough for a fresh start.
John had been pissed out of his head one night and shouting out the safe's combination, made her open the safe and count out the cash,
"You ever take so much as a penny and I will whore you until you fucking die, bitch" he threatened her. Laughing at her tears and promises of true love. Throughout all of that, she had remembered the combination.
'Laugh now, you cunt,' she thought.
For the last year and a half, she had shared this place with John. Spending most of her time, walking the grounds and the woods at the edge of the property, she knew just the place to hide the cash and diamonds, that were now wrapped in a bin bag. She made her way to the back of the house, out of the patio doors and across the grass that bordered the back of the garage, to the tree line that bordered open fields. There, she quickly found the wind felled tree that she often sat and had a fag on. The carcass of the tree lay slightly off the wet ground supported by snapped branches. She reached under, as far as she could and wedged the package tightly, covering it with loose soil and leaves. Twenty minutes later, she was back in bed. She would lie there, until a knock on the door from one of John's men roused her. They would make the fateful discovery together. He

would, no doubt, be off on his toes, leaving her to call the police and deal with the shitstorm that would follow. But deal with it she would, and in the following weeks, until she was made to leave the property, she would play the innocent, grieving girlfriend. She knew the BMW and Range Rover were in her name.

"Better in your name than mine," John had told her once. Hopefully the cops would allow her to keep them. All in all, if everything goes to plan, she might just leave with around quarter of a mill. 'I have earned every fucking penny,' she thought to herself. She spent the rest of the morning, until the banging on the door roused her, wondering who the hitman was and who John had crossed?

68

The drive to Scarbrough was uneventful. Tommy was driving in quite heavy traffic, so he simply kept pace, making space for drivers desperate to overtake, taking no risks. Bernie the Breaker was at the yard, waiting for Tommy. Within five minutes, the car had been relieved of its false number plates, picked up by a grab, dropped into the crusher, pressed into a cube and stacked with the other vehicle carcasses, ready for collection. Tommy showered and changed and burnt his clothing in a brazier. He shook Bernie's hand, passed him an envelope heavy with used £20 notes. He fired up the Bentley and headed off towards Whitby.

69

The drive to Hartlepool was pleasant. Tommy had checked in with Andrew and Pudding. Clive Ness was secure in the empty office space, that Gary Manners had lent to Tommy as a favour. There was no paper trail confirming this, simply one friend doing another a good turn. No cash had changed hands. Gary's friendship with Tommy was as strong as ever. He helped with securing premises as Tommy needed them and, once or twice a year, they had a boozy dinner together. If Tommy is doing something dodgy and he gets nicked, there was absolutely nothing, other than helping out a mate to tie Gary to Tommy. If he didn't get nicked, and he never had yet, then somewhere down the line there would be a cash thank you.

It took a little under 2 hours for Tommy to complete the journey. He parked next to a transit van, in the otherwise empty car park, and walked to the main entrance. The door opened before he needed to knock. Pudding grinned at him.

"All good boss?"

"Like clockwork," Tommy replied.

He made his way up a set of stairs, to what may have once been a board room or senior managers office. It now housed four laptops and half a dozen chairs, arranged around six scruffy, but serviceable, work stations that had been placed together to give the effect of a larger table. Andrew Leeson sat in one chair, Clive Ness in another. He had a bag over his head and was secured to his chair with tie wraps.

"Can we lose those Andrew," Tommy nodded to Clive Ness.

Seconds later, the bonds on Ness' wrists had been cut free and his head freed of the hood.

"Clive Ness, I'm Tommy Flounders, the man you were sent to kill. It's good to meet you at last." Tommy held out his hand. Ness, more than a little confused, shook it. "Now, before you go, I have a story I would like to tell you. Do you want tea or coffee?"

Ten minutes later, hot drinks and bacon butties in front of them, Tommy began.

"I don't know what you know about me, so here's a brief peek into my life. I run a number of successful businesses and the charity New Drill. One of my companies, Flounders and Partners, specialise in bespoke cyber security, supporting another company Titanium Security, as well as securing stand alone work. Flounders and Partners is staffed by brilliant, talented hackers, who spend all of their spare time at work in forums and chat rooms, keeping up to date with everything that is going on in the world of hacking. As a side line, these guys investigate other businesses and, on occasion, we tax medium or large cash rich companies by introducing ransomware to their IT systems.

This is how I became aware of John Jameson, and how your front company, Espien Accountants and Payrolls, became aware of me.

Firstly, to John Jameson. When we investigated his companies, we found that their turnover was massively inflated, compared to employees and their business models. Further investigation found that he ran a number of subscription and purchase by movie child porn sites, extreme BDSM, and even snuff sites. He was a people trafficker, often taking young women and putting them into his whore houses. Selling men to gang masters across the country, but particularly in Lincolnshire and Cambridgeshire where he has family ties. John dealt with all types of people, some of them wealthy and famous. He kept detailed records of those he thought could be useful, whether it was to help should he get into a hole or even for future extortion.

Once I had reviewed everything we could find, it was I, and I alone who decided that he was too evil to live. People like him are a pox on society and often, even when exposed, are able to avoid the punishments they so rightly deserve. We have put together a comprehensive suite of documents, which have now been anonymously forwarded to a number of Police forces across the country including Cambridgeshire, Essex, Greater Manchester, Lincolnshire and the 3 Yorkshire divisions. We have included as much detail as we can of his crime empire structure and his clients, including phone numbers, email addresses and purchase history.

I have little time for our police forces, in fact, for authority in general. I know a number of people on the list of subscribers will never be prosecuted. Money and sometimes simply who you are, will more often than not place you above the law. Are you with me so far?"

"Yes, I can't condone you taking a life outside of the law, but that does happen all too often. I could testify to that myself."

"Right, so on to Espien and how I came to your attention. We actually investigated your company as a possible target for ransomware activities. Nearly all money raised, by this side of the activity, is funnelled to New Drill, a charity that exists due to the apathy of successful government's that wash their hands of ex-service personnel, when they most need their support.

Our most junior hacker investigated your company. We have a strict policy of avoiding any Government or local authority companies. Local authorities are skint and government targets could bring too much heat down on us so we leave that to international operators. Once we realised that you were not a legitimate company, but a secret service cell, we exited your IT systems and moved on. Unfortunately, we left a footprint which was picked up and followed back to our servers.

I have to pay credit to your cybersecurity team, they accessed our systems and remain undetected for over 2 weeks, long enough to understand what we were about, and more specifically what my plans were for John Jameson. When we realised our security had been breached, we had to determine what to do. Very carefully, we accessed Espien again. This time, duplicating everything on your servers and analysing as much of the detail as possible. It was an incredibly stressful time. We had to work on, as if we had no idea that we had been compromised, meetings were arranged and held via handwritten notes. We had to leave mobile phones behind, never meeting in the office, whilst still doing our normal activity electronically, to avoid raising suspicions. Fortunately, through a contact, we were able to secure access to this building and gradually began to build a picture of Espien, all the time acting as if we were not aware that we were compromised.

My guys have a number of likeminded friends across the world. We were able to farm out some of the investigational work to them. What came back amazed and disappointed me. Essentially, your company is run by Alfred Smithe-Simpson. You work for the British government as a counter terrorist unit, specifically infiltrating and spying on groups and chat rooms, across the UK and sometimes further afield.

You work outside of the normal remit of UK law, from unauthorised phone tapping through to kidnap, torture and even murder, which is of course why we are sat here. Espien does not follow the usual protocol when reporting terrorist threats. Normally the various Secret Service divisions report to the Director General of security, who in turn reports to either the Foreign Secretary or the joint intelligence committee. The Foreign Secretary, Casper Trouton, went to Eton with Alfred Smithe-Simpson and they have remained firm friends ever since.

Because of the nature of Espien's work, reporting of activity is minimal. After all, if you are a MP, you don't really want to know someone is torturing and killing on your behalf. I'm guessing, you pretty much know all of this. Yes?"

"Yes"

"OK, well here's what you don't know. Despite coming from old money and having the best education money can buy, Casper Trouton, made significant investments as a young man. He risked, and all but lost, the family fortune. When he promoted Alfred to head of Espien, he did it on the understanding that three of your hackers would be diverted from their normal duties and would instead, break into and follow eight of the best fund managers and stock market investors in London and New York. Between Casper and Alfred, they appropriated £5,000,000 of funds destined to protect this country. They began to invest, based on, and following investments made by the aforementioned fund managers. These have proved very lucrative and they now hold over £30,000,000 between them. They hold the cash in crypto-currency accounts.

Let me explain, briefly, how it works. You purchase your currency through a crypto exchange. You can purchase it using conventional cash and exchange it back to conventional cash, when you choose to. It can then be stored in either a hot or cold wallet. A cold wallet is an offline method of storing someone's investment. It is pretty much infallible, as long as you do not lose the details of how to access your wallet and the public and private keys. A hot wallet is different in that it is an online storage system, for the public and private keys, both of which are necessary to allow the crypto currencies to be stored, purchased, sold and transferred. Both Casper and Alfred hold their currencies in hot wallets because these are much easier to use, when you may be making several transactions a week."

Tommy looked across the room to Terry.

"Did our transactions go well this morning?"

"Perfectly Tommy. We now hold all of the assets from both wallets in our own and will begin to fund New Drill with them, within a month."

"The problem with a hot wallet Clive is that if someone, say one of the best hackers in the world, were to come across the keys for the wallets, well they can simply strip the assets and walk away. Which is exactly what we have done.

Normally, even with crooked cunts like these two, we would have applied a tax of say 20% of assets, but with these I couldn't and here's the reason why.

In February of 2017, one of your surveillance officers raised a red flag report to Alfred. The details of the report were simple and frightening. An Islamic extremist, Salman Abedi, who would be helped by his brother Hashem Abedi, planned a suicide bomb attack in Manchester. WhatsApp messages and subsequent bugging of their telephones, showed the threat these two posed as very real.

When Alfred reported in the threat to Casper, instead of acting upon it, they decided to shut down the investigation, telling the operative that the surveillance had been passed to MI5, for follow up. What had in fact happened, was that between them both, they agreed to do nothing. Knowing that Casper could put pressure on the joint intelligence committee, to provide extra funding,

by saying that both Saman Abedi and Hashem Abedi had been identified by Espien but due to restrictive funds, they had been deemed as less of a risk than other larger cells and had not been followed up. Their plan went perfectly. The thought that a further £8,000,000 of government investment, could have saved all of these lives didn't sit easy with the government purse holders. What resulted was that funding was released and quickly passed to Espien, which in turn allowed Alfred to recruit another five operatives, one of which was destined to hack into further investment bankers. In short, Casper Trouton and Alfred Smithe-Simpson put personal gain, ahead of the lives of innocent children and parents."
"Are you sure of this?" asked Clive Ness.
"Perfectly, and here are some of the electronic communications that back it up." Tommy dropped a file of printed emails in front of Clive Ness.
"Pudding did the hit go well this morning?"
"Perfect Boss. In and out very cleanly. Should be home within two hours if the traffic's good."
"Cracker, has the communication reached and been read by Casper Trouton?"
"Yeah Tommy. He's fucking furious but so far has done exactly what he has been told"
"Whilst we were both busy this morning, I had another two operations going on. Alfred Smithe-Simpson was picked up, outside of his house in Wimbledon, eliminated and now lies in the boot of his Range Rover in a multi-storey car park. In a perfect world, Casper Trouton would have suffered a similar fate, but killing a cabinet minister would have been a step too far even for ourselves. So instead, we have contacted him, explained to him that all of his assets have been requisitioned and that his cohort is no longer an active member of Espien. We have planned out his day for him, up to his

resignation tonight, from his post and public office. Should he fail to comply, everything we have on him will be made public.

In a few hours, Alfred's body will be discovered. Casper Trouton will ensure MI5 will take over the investigation from the Metropolitan Police and that they will conclude it was a knife robbery gone wrong.

I have looked very carefully at you Clive and have no reason to believe you are anything other than, an honest, upright citizen. Which is the only reason you are still breathing. Casper Trouton's last task as Foreign Secretary, before he resigns, will be to appoint you as the new head of Espien. You can tell him everything we have discussed here, if you wish. If he moves against me, I will release every document we have on him and he will be ruined. Do you have any questions?"

"No, but I don't think Casper is the kind of guy to go quietly. He will look at every avenue to save his own skin. Making him resign is bad enough, but bankrupting him! You have made an enemy for life."

"Thanks for the warning, but I have had more enemies than hot dinners, and none have managed to lay a finger on me."

Tommy walked Clive down to a waiting car.

"You will be with your vehicle within two hours. I am putting a lot of faith in you Clive. An old buddy of mine will be turning in his grave knowing I have released you, but my gut says you are a good guy. Serve your country well."

"I don't really know what to say. You have pretty much turned my life upside down. Last chance I guess. Are you sure about doing everything you have done. It's not too late to give Casper something of the money he embezzled."

"Never. Fuck him and fuck everyone born to money, inbred worthless cunts that run this country and think the country owes them, and not the other way around."
With that final exchange, Tommy and Clive shook hands, Clive climbed into the car and was driven back to his car.

70

A little less than a year passed and Tommy's companies had flourished. New Drill prospered with the injection of money from 'mystery donors.' Terry had finally married and his wife, Yvonne, was expecting their first child. Tommy walked up the stairs of his house to the main living area, passed the lounge overlooking the sea and into the spacious well equipped kitchen. He stopped dead in his tracks. Seated at the kitchen island was Clive Ness and next to him, was a big, useful looking man holding a small revolver. A push in his back propelled Tommy past the door. Two more men, both armed, stood behind him.

"Take a seat please Tommy." Clive nodded his head towards a chair at the other side of the island. Tommy sat.

"I didn't expect to see you again Clive and judging by your company, this may not be too pleasant for me."

"My company are all currently special service personnel. I have briefed them on who you are and your links to New Deal. We are all grateful for your contribution to our colleagues, but they will not hesitate to act, unless you comply fully with me. You understand?"

"Yes. May I make a mug of tea?"

"Billy will do that, whilst we chat." One of the three men stood and put on a kettle"

"Tea bags are in the cupboard immediately in front of you," said Tommy, as if they were all old friends.

"Now Clive, what can I do for you?"

"I am here to give you a choice Tommy. A small injection behind an ear and a peaceful death. The coroner's report, that has already been written, will show a massive heart attack took you. Or, if you want to try to

take us on, to resist, you will simply disappear, which is for those who love you, far more messy.
Remember last time we met, I told you our mutual friend would carry a grudge. Well he still has enough friends in high places to carry it out. I am sure I was chosen to complete the task, as a warning to me as well. Old money, alliances born out of mutual greed, the wealthy keeping the poor in their place, all of these factors have brought me to your door, I am as much a victim of this as you."
"From your point of view maybe, but from mine, well maybe not so much." A mug of steaming black tea was put in front of Tommy, along with a pint of milk.
"I think I would like to go, looking out at the sea. Is that ok?"
"I'm sure we can accommodate that. If you behave and comply, I will do everything I can, to treat you with the courtesy you once treated me."
Tommy sipped his tea.
"Through that door, is a bathroom. There is only a small window, it has no vent. I would like to go take a shit and a piss, if that's ok. No man should be found, sitting in his own waste."
"Billy, would you go check it out please. Tommy empty your pockets. We don't want anything like a phone call to complicate things."
Tommy emptied his pockets, wallet, keys, phone, all set on the island.
"That's all I have. No phone calls, no drama, you have my word on that, and my word means something to me," he said, pointedly looking directly at Clive.
Ten minutes later, Tommy sat in a wing backed leather chair, looking out at Hartlepool Bay. It was dark outside. The lights of ships and the wind turbines, twinkled in the darkness.

There were no lights on in Tommy's lounge.
"Talk me through it then Clive."
"As I said earlier, a small injection and you pass. No drama, no fuss. We will have to hold you in place. Some men, when faced with death, seem to think they can cheat it at the last minute. Also, you may spasm for a second or two. Are you ready Tommy?"
"Not sure it makes any difference one way or another. Take a tight hold guys and don't snap that fucking needle."
Clive put a syringe to the back of Tommy's ear. Tommy spasmed, his body going rigid, his back arching out of the chair. The last thing he saw was the lights of a harbour master vessel, traveling from Hartlepool towards the River Tees, then his eyes finally closed.

71

Tommy had covert surveillance equipment installed in every room in his house. Either cameras and microphones or just microphones. Everything was motion or sound activated, and stored on a server at Flounders and Partners on a seventy two hour loop. Only he, Terry and Cracker knew about this, and only the 3 of them could access the server.

He knew he had made a number of enemies over the years, and reasoned a hit in his house was most likely. If this were to happen, any detail that could be made available, would help protect his team and if possible, allow them to right the wrong.

Within hours of Terry discovering Tommy's body, after he had failed to come in to work or answer his phone, Terry, Cracker, Pudding and Andrew, the closest of Tommy's friends, sat reviewing the tape, time after time. Anger filled the room and revenge was needed. Clive Ness, Casper Trouton and anyone else involved needed to be killed, yet they could not act.

When Tommy had gone to take that last bathroom break, he said the following.

"Right guys, listen up and listen hard. Do nothing. Do absolutely nothing until the day after the funeral. It's important you wait. I have trusted all of you since I have known you, please trust me with this."

He then flushed the toilet and joined Clive Ness, for his remaining minutes.

"What the fuck difference will the funeral make?" said Pudding, voicing what everyone was thinking. Cracker spoke up,

"Tommy has always been one step ahead of the game. Let's just wait and see."

"Being dead isn't one step ahead of any fucking thing!" said Andrew.

"Nevertheless, we wait," said the new chairman of Tommy's businesses, Terry. We all want revenge. Think about it, every waking moment if you want. Plan it out in your heads but do nothing, until the funeral is done."

72

The funeral was a sombre affair, not the celebration that Jacko had had. Tommy had requested friends and family only. Despite having no living relatives, Tommy considered his closest friends as family. After a short service and burial in Stranton cemetery, a wake was hosted by Mike and Jackie at the Drunken Duck, a thriving pub that had become Tommy's favourite not far from his house.
A more rowdy wake would take place the following Saturday, at Catterick Camp.
Terry was sat with Cracker and Yvonne when a scruffy looking old man wandered over to him.
"You Terry?" he asked. "Yes, I am. What can I do for you?"
"I'm Brian Long, I have known Tommy since before he had fucking pubes. It was me that arranged to get his hands fixed up years ago. He asked me to hold this for his funeral and give it to you. So there you are." Brian passed an envelope to Terry. "I like single malt whiskey, if you're wondering," he said, as he wandered towards the bar. Cracker rose and put £50 in Brians hand.
"Thanks fella. Don't mind getting your own, do you?"
"Nah. I aint got nothin better to do, I suppose."
Terry opened and read the contents of the envelope. He passed it to Cracker, Pudding and Andrew in turn. Each of them reading the following: -
'I hope by the time you have finished reading this, you understand why I couldn't let you know what was going to happen. On 15th October, Clive Ness reached out to me. He told me that I was to be terminated, that Casper Trouton had pulled enough strings with his old buddies, for me to be killed. Clive had argued against this but was reminded that there was more than one agency that was

capable of carrying out such tasks, and that his status and loyalty may be questioned if he didn't comply.
Clive is a decent man, he offered me the opportunity to disappear,
Korea, Chile, Japan, Bali, anywhere out of Europe and the USA. I would have been safe to live my life out, in relative comfort. I didn't for one minute consider this. I have lived and loved my life in Hartlepool. I couldn't imagine being alive and being remote from you all. I would be a man in hiding, on the run. Always looking over my shoulder. That's no way to live life.
I also had to consider Clive. He would surely have compromised himself should I just up sticks and disappear. There was always a chance that sometime, my past would catch up with me. I went to my death in peace, knowing that I have made greater friends, had better times than I could ever have hoped for, when I started running with a wild man called Billy the Scouse when I was just 14 years old. I have met too many men to name but I have considered my friends but you four. Terry, Cracker, Pudding and Andrew, along with my dearest friend Jacko, have enriched my life, more than I could ever have imagined. So thank you all.
Now to some practical stuff. I believe that the board room, or even Titanium security, may have been breached. Because of this, I want you all to meet at my house tomorrow, to discuss the future of the companies. No phones with you that day. In fact, I would say park up in and around Seaton. Leave your phones in your cars and walk to my gaff, alone, not in a group. Once there, you can decide how to move on.
Tommy'

73

The following afternoon at 12.30, Pudding was last to arrive. Terry had been first, part of his inheritance was Tommy's house. He was yet to decide whether to move into it or not, but it would make a great family home. He had been grilling bacon and making butties. The coffee percolator was full to the brim and a huge pot of tea sat on the table in the kitchen diner. Everyone was just tucking into a sandwich and having a drink before discussing recent events and the contents of Tommy's letter.
Just as Terry sat down, the doorbell went, the room went quiet.
"It's ok fella's," said Terry, "I've been expecting someone. Tuck in, I won't be a sec." Moments later, Terry walked back up the stairs followed by Clive Ness and the 3 servicemen that had accompanied him on that fateful day, a little over 2 weeks ago.
"What the fuck!" shouted Pudding, who was first to his feet, striding quickly around the table. The man next to Clive pulled a small pistol from his jacket.
"Sit, you cunt," he said menacingly. Pudding Sat.
"Terry, please don't tell me you have turned" said Cracker, a look of dismay on his face.
"No he hasn't" said Tommy, walking through to the kitchen from the lounge. "He has done exactly what I asked."
Tommy stood in the doorway. his salt and pepper hair shaved off, a full beard covered his once, always clean shaven face, blue contact lens' through plain lens, heavy black nerd glasses to finish off the disguise. The room was stunned. Andrew simply said "fuck!" Pudding, for once, lost for words, it was left to Cracker, who was always the most emotional of the group, to run and hug

Tommy, like a long lost father. With that, everyone was on their feet, hugging Tommy, shouting questions, living in a moment of pure joy.

"OK guys. Sit down and make room for Clive and his men. They saved my life, not killed me. I have a story to tell."

Everyone seated, Tommy began. "Not many weeks after we released Clive, he reached out to me. Our plan had worked, Casper Trouton had resigned, Clive had been promoted, but there were rumours coming back to Clive, that I was going to have to be disposed of. As a lesson for anyone like me, that the establishment will not be fucked with. Not only that, but it became clear to Clive, that part of Espien's functionality was to clean up after the rich and powerful, including two names on the list of subscribers, we provided to the police from John Jameson's list of paedophiles.

Since that day, we have worked together to bring us all around this table. With Clive are Billy, Phil and Kevin, all serving special forces personnel, Clive has pretty much known them since their enlistment. He trusts them, as much as I trust you. Within ten weeks, all will have retired and all will take roles within Espien. My death certificate is real, I am dead and buried. I used Marron brothers, undertakers. Many years ago, I got them out of a financial hole. These guys will take my secret to the grave with them.

Clive has provided me with a new identity and shortly, I will be moving to a place called Thrapston. So fucking far from the sea, it's criminal, but it has great road links South and North. As far as Clive can tell, there is no one living there that will recognise me. The five of us, are going to work to take down the worst of the scum, that lead a protected life. If we can, we will do it by exposing their crimes and perverse lives, or if we have to, by the

bullet. We start with the 2 pedo's that didn't fall with John Jameson.
What I would like you to do, is support that. You will pretty much go straight from now on, apart from piggybacking those bankers. Keep a very low profile, on occasion, I will call on you for support, hacking or otherwise. This is it lads, this is the last time we will ever get together like this. I will probably see you all occasionally, but get use to me not being around.
Now are you in, because if you are, we are going to be busy, very fucking quickly? Like next week quickly."

The End

Authors note
If, like me, you are unhappy at the way ex-service personnel are treated, by successive governments, there are a number of charities that exist to help them. My favourite is the Royal British Legion online shop - www.poppyshop.org.uk Give it a look if you can.

Email: tommythethinker@outlook.com

Printed in Great Britain
by Amazon